The only thing that kept him
sane was the thought of saving
his mother. But he could not
do one thing without the other.
Revenge and rescue. The bitter
truth was that he needed
them both.

Books by Simon Scarrow

GLADIATOR: FIGHT FOR FREEDOM
GLADIATOR: STREET FIGHTER
GLADIATOR: SON OF SPARTACUS
GLADIATOR: VENGEANCE

SIMON SCARROW

GLADIATOR
VENGEANCE

PUFFIN

PUFFIN BOOKS

Published by the Penguin Group

Penguin Books Ltd, 80 Strand, London WC2R ORL, England

Penguin Group (USA) Inc., 375 Hudson Street, New York, New York 10014, USA

Penguin Group (Canada), 90 Eglinton Avenue East, Suite 700, Toronto, Ontario, Canada M4P 2Y3
(a division of Pearson Penguin Canada Inc.)

Penguin Ireland, 25 St Stephen's Green, Dublin 2, Ireland (a division of Penguin Books Ltd)

Penguin Group (Australia), 707 Collins Street, Melbourne, Victoria 3008, Australia
(a division of Pearson Australia Group Pty Ltd)

Penguin Books India Pvt Ltd, 11 Community Centre, Panchsheel Park, New Delhi – 110 017, India

Penguin Group (NZ), 67 Apollo Drive, Rosedale, Auckland 0632, New Zealand
(a division of Pearson New Zealand Ltd)

Penguin Books (South Africa) (Pty) Ltd, Block D, Rosebank Office Park, 181 Jan Smuts Avenue,
Parktown North, Gauteng 2193, South Africa

Penguin Books Ltd, Registered Offices: 80 Strand, London WC2R ORL, England

puffinbooks.com

Published in Great Britain in Puffin Books 2014

001

Text copyright © Simon Scarrow, 2014
Map by David Atkinson
Map copyright © Penguin Books Ltd, 2014

The moral right of the author and illustrator has been asserted

Set in 11/18.5 pt Bembo Book MT Std
Typeset by Palimpsest Book Production Limited, Falkirk, Stirlingshire
Printed in Great Britain by Clays Ltd, St Ives plc

British Library Cataloguing in Publication Data
A CIP catalogue record for this book is available from the British Library

ISBN: 978-0-141-33903-0

www.greenpenguin.co.uk

MIX
Paper from
responsible sources
FSC
www.fsc.org   FSC™ C018179

Penguin Books is committed to a sustainable
future for our business, our readers and our planet.
This book is made from Forest Stewardship
Council™ certified paper.

To John O'Leary and Anita Gentry
who read the very first work . . .

1

'Ready?' asked Festus.

Marcus nodded and then glanced round the marketplace of Chalcis, a small port on the coast of the Gulf of Corinth. Below the market the ground sloped down to the sea, brilliant blue beneath the clear sky and the glare of early afternoon sun. They had reached the town after a morning's walk along the coastal road, then stopped for a simple meal of stew in a chop house to one side of the market. A fair-sized crowd was still milling around the stalls and the usual gangs of youths clustered about the fountain, presenting easy pickings to Marcus's practised eye.

'Do we have to do this?' asked Lupus, the boy sitting next to Marcus. He was seventeen, four years older than Marcus, but they often passed for the same age. Whereas Lupus was short and thin, Marcus was tall for his years. The hard training he had endured at a gladiator school, and later in the charge of Festus when they had both served Julius Caesar in Rome, had given him a muscular physique.

Festus turned to Lupus with a weary sigh. 'You know we do. The money Caesar gave us will not last forever. Better that we make it stretch by earning whatever we can along the way. Who knows how long it will take to find out where Marcus's mother is being held prisoner.'

Marcus felt a stab of pain in his heart. It had been over two years since he last saw her, when they were torn apart following the murder of Titus, the man Marcus had thought was his father. They had lived happily, on a farm on the island of Leucas, until the day when Titus could not repay a moneylender. A ruthless gang of men had come to seize the family and sell them into slavery to pay off Titus's debt. The old soldier had tried to resist but was killed, along with Marcus's dog, Cerberus, and Livia and Marcus were condemned to slavery. Marcus had escaped and, ever since, had vowed to find his mother and set her free.

At first it had seemed an impossible task, but, after saving Caesar's life, the great Roman statesman had given him a small sum of silver and a letter of introduction, together with the services of Festus, Caesar's most trusted bodyguard, and Lupus, and set him free to save his mother. They had sailed to Greece with two other men, both sent back to Rome by Festus when it became clear that Caesar's money would run out far too quickly with more mouths to feed.

After landing in Greece, the three of them took the coast road along the north of the Gulf as they made for Stratos, where Marcus had first encountered Decimus, the moneylender who had caused him so much grief and suffering. Along the route they had paid their way by putting on a small performance in the towns and ports they passed through.

Festus pushed his empty bowl away and stood up, stretching his shoulders and neck. 'On your feet, lads. It's time for the show.'

Marcus and Lupus rose from the bench and picked up their bags. They contained a few spare clothes and a handful of personal belongings – writing materials in the case of Lupus, and an assortment of weapons for Marcus and Festus. Festus dipped into his purse and tossed a few bronze asses on the table to cover the cost of their meal, then gestured for the two boys to follow him. They emerged from the inn's weathered canopy into the glare of the sun and made their way across the square to the fountain. It was late April and the mountain streams were full so there was still sufficient flow from the water piped into the port to feed the fountain. A steady rush overflowed the central cupola and splashed down into the round basin beneath, cooling the air immediately around the fountain. Which is why it was the favourite haunt of the gangs of youths, and the toughs who hired their services out to landlords and moneylenders. Just the kind of people Festus was looking for.

The fountain was surrounded by a shallow flight of steps, just enough for a man standing at the top to be clearly seen above the crowd in the market square. Festus set his bag down and the others followed suit.

'Keep an eye on them,' Festus told Lupus. Then he turned to Marcus. 'Let's do it.'

They stepped up to the edge of the fountain and Festus raised his hands and drew a deep breath before calling out to the crowd in Greek.

'Friends! Hear me! Hear me!'

Faces turned towards the fountain as people stopped to stare, their curiosity aroused. The groups of men round the fountain stopped their idle banter and glared at the man and boy who had disturbed their daily routine. There would be no shortage of volunteers to take up the challenge that Festus was about to make.

'Noble people of Chalcis!' Festus continued. 'You are the heirs of the proud tradition of the heroic Greeks who once took on and defeated the great empire of Persia. More recently, alas, you have fallen before the might of Rome and they – we – are now your masters.'

He paused to allow some angry shouts of defiance from the small crowd gathering in front of the fountain. Marcus had grown up among the Greeks and knew how proud they were of their civilization. They bitterly resented being under the thumb of Romans whom they considered their inferiors and Festus was very deliberately playing on this, making sure he spoke with a marked Roman accent when he addressed them again.

'No doubt there are many men here who still hold true to the warrior spirit of their forebears.'

'Yes!' One of the toughs standing a short distance away shouted back. 'And you'll find that out quick enough if you carry on opening your trap!'

There was a chorus of support from his cronies.

'Push off, Roman!' the tough continued with a menacing grin. 'And take your little runts with you.'

Festus turned to the man with a beaming smile. 'Ah! I see that I was right about the people of Chalcis. There are still one or two real men living here.'

'More than that, Roman!' another heavy-set man responded. 'Now do as he says, and get out of here, before we make you.'

Festus raised his hands and called for quiet. It took a while before those in the crowd hurling insults and threats fell silent. But most of the townspeople were keen to see what would come next and they hushed the others.

'I meant no offence!' Festus called out. 'We are merely travellers passing through your lands. My name is Festus. I have angered you, and for that I apologize most humbly. But it seems that there are some here for whom an apology is not enough.'

'How right you are, Roman!' the first tough shouted back as his companions cheered him.

Festus faced the man directly. 'In which case, it only seems fair that I give you a chance to teach us a lesson.' He turned to Marcus. 'Time for the training staffs.'

Marcus nodded and bent to open his goatskin pack, taking out a small bundle of wooden staffs, each five foot in length and thicker than a man's thumb. He passed one to Festus who held it up for all to see.

'Who will take on me and the boy in a contest to see who can stay on their feet longest?'

'Me!' The tough thumped his chest, and several others joined in as they stepped towards Festus. 'Andreas is my name. And I'll give you such a hiding that you will never forget it!'

'Very good!' Festus replied. 'A contest we shall have. But let's keep it fair. Four of you against the two of us.'

The tough laughed scornfully. 'Done! It's time you stuck-up Romans were taught a hard lesson. Four against you, and your runt. You'll take a beating and no mistake. Of course, if you want to beg my forgiveness, then I might just let you walk out of Chalcis in one piece. Providing you hand your packs over to us first. Spoils of war, Roman. You'd know all about that, I'm sure.'

'I wouldn't dream of denying you the pleasure of humbling us,' Festus replied smoothly. 'But let's make this even more interesting.'

He reached down and took out his purse and held it up. 'I'll wager ten pieces of silver that the boy and I win. Who'll take the bet?'

There was a moment's hesitation as the townspeople took in the new development and then a well-dressed merchant in a blue tunic raised his arm. 'I'll take the bet. I'll match your silver if you take on Andreas and his comrades.' He pointed to the tough.

The latter nodded eagerly. 'Done! Here, Eumolpus, you're with me.' He turned to look at the nearest gang of youths and stabbed his finger at two of the larger boys. 'Thrapsus and you,

Atticus. You deal with the Roman whelp while we give this loudmouth a hiding. Now let's have those little sticks of yours, Roman, and set to it!'

'Be my guest.' Festus nodded to Marcus, who stepped forward and held out the staffs for the Greeks to select their weapons. Andreas took the first to hand and then three more, which he passed to the men he had selected. Marcus and Festus took the remaining two from the bundle that Festus had prepared with wood cut from trees along the road for this purpose.

'Clear a space there!' Festus stepped down from the fountain into the square and swept his staff out to urge the crowd back. They shuffled away and when he had cleared a space thirty feet across Festus stepped into the middle, hefting his staff, as Marcus strode over and took up his position, back to back. Raising his staff, Marcus held it out in both hands, horizontally. As always before a fight, he felt his heart quicken and his muscles tense. Andreas and his comrades spread out round them, the men facing Festus, and the two youths taking on Marcus. He cast his eyes over them quickly, assessing each boy.

The one called Thrapsus was thickset with lank hair tied back by a leather thong. His face was mottled with angry spots and when he bared his teeth they were stained and crooked.

8

His companion, Atticus, was taller, and took rather more care of his appearance. His hair was neatly cut and his tunic, while plain, was clean and fitted his sinewy body neatly. His features were fine, like one of the many statues of young athletes that Marcus had seen in the towns they had passed through since landing in Greece. No doubt he fancied himself as something of a ladies' man, Marcus guessed.

'Same as before,' Festus growled over his shoulder. 'We cover each other's back and make it look good. Give the crowd a bit of a show before we put these thugs down on the ground. Got that?'

'I know what I have to do,' Marcus muttered back. 'You've trained me well enough. Let's just get on with it.'

Festus turned to wink at him. 'Always spoiling for a fight, ain't you? That's the spirit.'

Marcus pressed his lips together. In truth he hated fighting. He hated the sick feeling in the pit of his stomach. The only thing that drove him on was the thought of rescuing his mother. That was why he fought. That was the only reason.

'Ready?' asked Festus.

'Ready.'

Festus looked at the tough. 'Let's begin!'

2

At first no one moved. Marcus and Festus stood back to back, watching their opponents closely, looking for any sign that gave away an imminent attack. Marcus noted that Thrapsus was holding his staff in both hands like a club, half raised, ready to swing at Marcus. By contrast the other youth seemed to have some idea of how to use a staff in a fight and had it grasped with his hands apart so that he could jab with the ends, or block any blows as strongly as possible.

He heard Festus's sandals scrape over the flagstones and he glanced back to see his companion easing himself upright and laying his staff across a shoulder as he mocked the two men facing him.

'What's the problem, my friends? Lost the stomach for an easy fight?'

'You talk too much,' Andreas growled. 'Won't be so easy when I knock your teeth out, Roman.'

He did not wait for a response but let out a loud roar and charged at Festus, swinging his staff at the latter's head in a vicious arc. An instant later his three companions also charged in, echoing his cry. Marcus's gaze snapped back to the two youths as he left Festus to fight his own battle. That was the plan. Each trusted the other to hold his own and guard his comrade's back. Atticus held back and let his sturdier friend charge in first. Thrapsus raised the stick above his head, fully extending his arms to get as much power into the blow as possible. Marcus shifted his left hand back as he turned the end of the stick towards the Greek boy and punched it forward into his chest, just below his chin. The impact stopped Thrapsus in his tracks and he stumbled back, gasping for breath as he lowered his staff and dropped a hand to clutch at his chest. Marcus took a step forward and lowered the point of his staff and struck again, this time aiming for his opponent's stomach.

He avoided aiming for the face and groin, just as Festus instructed. The object of the exercise was not to cause any lasting injuries and the bad feeling that went with them. A simple lesson was all that was required; enough to put them out of the fight so that only their dignity would be hurt. Thrapsus staggered back from the blow, completely winded now and struggling to breathe. Marcus lowered the staff again and stabbed into the ground behind the youth's heel, then barged forward with his shoulder. Thrapsus lost his balance and fell heavily on to the ground, the staff flying from his grip and clattering a short distance away.

The local boy's defeat had been so quick that it took a moment for the spectators to grasp what had happened and then many of them groaned with disappointment. There were a few muted cries of support for Marcus and he realized that the thuggish young man was not popular with all of the port's inhabitants. He recovered his staff and retreated towards Festus, a background of grunts and the clatter of wood sounding in his ears as he concentrated his attention on the second youth. Atticus had looked stunned by the ease with which his companion had gone down and now a cold, ruthless look fixed on his expression as he lowered himself into a crouch and glared at Marcus.

'A pretty neat move, Roman,' he said through gritted teeth. 'But you won't find me as much of a fool as that oaf Thrapsus.'

Marcus shrugged. 'We'll see. But a word of advice. Save your breath. You'll need it.'

Atticus's dark eyebrows knitted in anger and he leaned down

12

to snatch up the staff lying on the floor and then advanced, swinging one cane in each hand. *An unusual technique*, Marcus thought quickly to himself, *but not a terribly effective one*. While Atticus would be able to bombard him with a flurry of blows, they would not have as much force behind them as a properly wielded weapon. As he expected, the Greek came on swinging the staffs wildly, swishing through the air as he sought to strike the Roman boy. Marcus held his staff up and flicked it right and left to parry the blows in a succession of sharp cracks as wood struck wood.

He was mindful of the other instruction that Festus had given him: to try and make the fight against his second opponent last a little longer. It would save the crowd from being disappointed. Give them value for money, Festus had said. That's what a good gladiator does. And, when it was over, the crowd would have had their fill of excitement and the losing fighters would feel that they had put up a decent show and their pride, while dented, would be enhanced by the thought that they had sorely tested their winning opponent.

Marcus mixed a few feints in between his parries, forcing the Greek boy back, and after several more attacks Atticus retreated out of range, breathing hard as he stared at Marcus, his staffs trembling with the effort of holding them out. Hearing a deep grunt behind, Marcus risked a glance round and saw that Festus had felled one of the men who lay sprawled across the flagstones, out cold. He turned back to Atticus, confident that now it was one-on-one he no longer had to stay so close to Festus. Slipping his left hand back a short distance, Marcus lowered the end of the staff and grasped it like a spear as he stepped forward.

Atticus slashed at the end of the staff, knocking it aside, but, each time, Marcus aimed the point at his face again and took another pace towards him, forcing him back towards the crowd. The Greek youth was weakening and at last he gathered his wits enough to realize he would have more control over a single staff. He drew back his right hand and hurled the staff at Marcus. The length of wood spun through the air and Marcus felt a sharp pain as one end caught him above the ear before he could duck. He felt a warm trickle down the side of his neck and his opponent let out a cry of triumph as he saw the blood, charging forward and slashing from side to side, his remaining staff held in both hands.

Marcus retreated two steps and held his ground, deflecting the wild blows, sensing the trembling in the other boy's limbs as it transmitted itself from staff to staff. Atticus was tiring, and desperate to put an end to the fight. There was another sharp exchange of blows, the clatter echoing off the tall walls of a

14

temple standing close to the fountain. Then Marcus leapt forward, bunching his muscles as he made a vicious cut at the knuckles of the Greek. The wood smacked down on the bone and Atticus let out a cry of agony and snatched his injured hand back, releasing his grip. At once the balance of his weapon was lost and the end wavered. Marcus pressed his staff against it and then swirled the end round and flicked his arms up, snatching the staff from the other boy's hand and sending it up into the air, end over end. The crowd let out a gasp of surprise and admiration, but the contest wasn't over yet. Marcus had to put his opponent down.

Atticus was as shocked as the spectators, too shocked to react as Marcus rushed up to him, planted his boot down behind the other boy's leg and thrust his staff hard into his midriff. Just like his stockier comrade, Atticus went flying, landing heavily on his back. At once Marcus punched his staff into the air and cried out.

'Victory!'

'No!' Atticus gasped painfully and began to struggle up.

Marcus quickly lowered his staff and poked the end into the other boy's chest, just below his throat, pressing him back. 'A word of advice. When you are down, stay down. Or face the consequences.' He gave the staff an extra nudge to emphasize his point. With a fierce scowl, Atticus nodded and raised his hands in defeat.

Marcus turned round to see how Festus was doing. He was squaring up to Andreas, and the Greek, in turn, was standing, legs braced as he held his staff in a firm two-handed grip, ready to counter any move that Festus made.

'Need any help?' asked Marcus.

'No. This one's all mine.'

Andreas snorted and shook his head. 'By the Gods, you must fancy yourself! Typical bloody Roman.' His chest was heaving as he gasped for breath. He was a big man, Marcus observed. But he was out of condition, unlike Festus who exercised every day and whose body was as quick as his mind. Festus shaped to make a fresh attack and lunged with his staff, aiming for the other man's stomach. But Andreas, heavy and unfit as he was, had the reflexes of a cat and knocked the staff aside before countering with a jab at the Roman, which caught him a glancing blow off the ribs. Festus drew back and winced as he felt his side. He bowed a quick salute to his opponent, then took a long, deep breath and grasped his staff firmly again.

Marcus felt a stab of concern for his friend but knew better than to intervene. Festus was a proud man, and any attempt to help him would only incur his anger. So Marcus lowered his staff and stood aside. Since he was the first to complete his fight there was one other task that fell to him. He looked around for the merchant who had taken the bet but could not see him immediately. Then he noticed a flash of blue and saw him edging towards the rear of the crowd. Returning his staff to his pack, Marcus drew out a dagger and tucked it inside the wide leather belt fastened round his midriff. He took another glance at Festus and saw him moving forward to renew the fight. Andreas raised his staff high, aiming for the Roman's face, but Festus did not flinch. He thrust at the Greek and as his opponent moved to parry the blow, Festus cut under his staff, angled his weapon down and jabbed it at the Greek's foot, crushing his toes.

Andreas bellowed in pain and instinctively lifted his injured foot to hop back, while still keeping his staff held up to counter his Roman opponent. It was too much for the heavy-set man to coordinate and he stumbled and fell, grunting as the air was driven from his lungs. Festus whacked the staff out of his hands and then pressed the end into the other man's guts. Many in the crowd let out whoops of laughter as they saw the tough's clumsy fall and Andreas flushed angrily.

'Yield,' Festus demanded.

The Greek's expression darkened and then he glanced

17

quickly round the crowd and realized that most were cheering for Festus and laughing in good humour. He forced himself to smile as he struggled painfully to his feet and held out his hand.

'You won fairly, Roman. Chalcis has rarely seen a fighter like you. It is no dishonour to be bested by a professional fighter. A gladiator, perhaps?'

'Once,' Festus conceded, shifting his staff to his left hand and cautiously clasping hands with the Greek. 'Now, I am merely a traveller in your land.'

'And the boy? Surely too young to be a gladiator as well?'

'No. He was a gladiator before he won his freedom.'

'Really?' Andreas looked round, and frowned. 'Now where in Hades has he got to?'

Already halfway through the crowd, most of whom ignored him as their attention was occupied by Festus, Marcus was heading steadily in the direction of the blue tunic he had seen a moment earlier. The crowd began to thin out as he reached the rows of stalls and he saw the merchant walking quickly towards a street that led away from the market. Marcus ducked into a parallel street a short distance away and broke into a run. When he reached the first junction, he turned towards the street the merchant had gone down, then sprinted down a narrow alley towards the next corner where he stopped and pressed himself against the rough plaster of the wall. He drew his dagger from his belt and tried to breathe as quietly as possible when he heard the soft slap of sandals approaching. A moment later the merchant passed by him and Marcus stepped out, pressing the point of his knife into the small of the man's back.

The merchant let out a yelp of surprise and turned as he backed against the building opposite.

'You have a wager to honour, if I'm not mistaken,' Marcus smiled. 'Now let's go back to the market to settle the matter. Ten pieces of silver. You'd better be good for it or my friend Festus is going to be unhappy.'

The merchant swiftly recovered from his surprise and his lips curled in contempt as he stared at Marcus. 'You're nothing more than a boy. Get out of my way.'

Marcus stepped to the side to block his path. 'I'm the boy who just beat two of your street thugs in a fight. I'm also the boy who is holding a knife no more than a foot from your stomach. Now, you have a debt to pay. Back to the market. Move.'

'That's nine . . . Ten.' The merchant counted the silver coins into Festus's palm.

19

'I thank you,' Festus smiled. 'And next time it might be an idea not to try and slip away.'

'There won't be a next time, I trust,' the merchant replied sourly. 'I hope I never set eyes on you, or your nasty little sidekick, ever again.'

'You'd better hope that you don't.' Festus rested his hand on Marcus's shoulder. 'Or next time I think my friend Marcus might not feel so willing to hold back with his dagger.'

'He wouldn't dare!' The merchant spat in contempt.

Marcus tilted his head to the side. 'No? Want to put it to the test?'

The merchant retreated and then hurriedly recovered his composure. 'Bah! A bunch of petty con men, the pair of you. I've a good mind to report you to the town magistrates.'

'Why don't you?' Festus dared him. 'I'm sure they'd be interested in a man who tried to avoid paying a bet he made witnessed by everyone in the market of Chalcis.'

The merchant let out a hiss of bitter frustration and turned to hurry across the market square. The crowd that had gathered to watch the fight had dispersed and Marcus, Festus and Lupus packed away the remaining staffs. Andreas, sitting on the steps of the fountain to nurse his foot, chuckled as the merchant strode away.

'Ah, forget him. There are plenty of men like Clysto around. They deserve what's coming to them.' The Greek stood up slowly to test his weight on his foot and winced.

'Sorry about that,' said Festus. 'But I had to put you down quickly after that blow to the ribs.'

'On another day I'd have knocked you down, Roman.'

'If you say so.'

'I do . . . You and your boys thirsty?'

Festus glanced round and both Lupus and Marcus nodded.

'Good!' Andreas approached and rested his hand on Marcus's shoulder. 'And as for you, boy, you are just as fierce as your friend Festus. By the Gods, if I had ten of you in my gang I'd rule the streets of this town. Come with me. I know a good place to drink. And I'm paying.'

3

'How's the foot?' asked Festus as he set his cup down with a sharp rap on the table.

'Sore.' Andreas replied and then grinned. 'How's your side?'

'Sore.'

They both laughed and Andreas reached for the jug to top up their cups, and then after a moment's thought, poured a little more of the watered wine into the cups of Marcus and Lupus. The inn the Greek had chosen had been up a steep side street that led to a small plateau. Built on the edge of a cliff, it overlooked the town and the sparkling sea beyond. A light breeze cooled them after the hot confines of the market and there was a faint rustling from the branches of a cedar tree that provided shade for the customers.

'You, boy.' Andreas looked squarely at Marcus. 'You fight

like a demon. I only saw snatches of it while I was dealing with your friend here, but what I saw was impressive. Your gladiator school must have been one of the best. I've seen a few fights in the theatre here, but it was rough stuff compared to the show you two put on. Where are you from, exactly?'

Marcus raised his cup in thanks and took a sip of the vinegary brew before he replied. 'I was trained at a school near Capua. And then by Festus when I was bought by a new master and taken to Rome.'

'And you?' Andreas turned to Lupus. 'What's your story? You don't look the kind of lad who should be in the company of two trained killers.'

'We're not killers,' Festus said evenly. 'Our job was to protect our master.'

'Master? I thought you said that you had been freed? Marcus at least.'

Festus smiled thinly. 'Force of habit. I was set free some years ago and stayed with my . . . employer. Marcus was given his liberty several months back. A reward for good service. Lupus too.'

'Then he's a fighter as well?' Andreas looked doubtful as he ran his eyes over Lupus's slight physique. 'I can't see it. He wouldn't last a moment in a fight.'

'I can fight!' Lupus shot back defiantly. 'When I have to.'

The Greek chuckled and held up one of his big hands to pacify the smaller boy. 'I meant no offence, my little friend. Just an observation. Unless my eyes are deceived your skills lie outside the art of fighting. Am I right?'

Lupus flushed and raised his chin proudly. 'I am a scribe, by training. I can read, write and do calculations. As good as any man.'

Andreas laughed. 'I am sure. But outside of a merchant's house, or in the service of some aristocrat, your usefulness is, er, somewhat limited.'

Marcus leaned forward. 'Lupus is my friend. I trust him with my life. That is all that you need to know about him.'

It was true. Marcus did indeed trust him with his life. Lupus knew the secret of his birth and the meaning of the scar on his shoulder where he had been branded as an infant to show that he was the son of Spartacus. Lupus had given his most sacred promise to keep it to himself. But Festus did not know. Nor could he ever know, Marcus decided. However close the bond between them, Festus had been with Caesar long before Marcus had entered his life. It would be dangerous to test his loyalty to his former master. Festus was a man of honour and unbending in the principles he believed in. He had been ordered by Caesar to accompany Marcus on his quest to find and save his mother. If he discovered that Marcus was the son of Spartacus, one of the most dangerous enemies ever to have threatened Rome, then he would feel duty-bound to inform Caesar and obey any instructions that Caesar gave to decide the fate of Marcus.

Andreas leaned back from the table and cast a sympathetic look at Festus. 'A touchy pair, these two. How do you put up with them? If they were in my charge, I'd give 'em a good clip round the ear if they opened their mouths like that.'

'They're not in my charge,' Festus replied. 'They are my companions. My comrades in arms. My friends.'

It was the first time that Festus had used the word and both Marcus and Lupus looked at him in surprise. Marcus felt a surge of pride that this man he admired and respected should regard him as a friend. Despite all the dangers and hardships they had shared, Festus had never revealed his feelings.

'Friends, eh?' Andreas cocked an eyebrow. 'So what are you and your friends doing here, far from Rome? I assume there's more to it than wandering from town to town, earning a pittance from your fights.'

'It pays for food and lodging,' Festus countered. 'What more do we need?'

'What indeed?' Andreas took a gulp of wine and ran his eyes

25

over each of them in turn before he continued. 'So, what's the real story?'

Marcus knew that if they were to succeed in their quest then they would need information. He exchanged a quick look with Festus and nodded subtly.

'We're looking for someone,' said Festus. 'Maybe you can help us.'

'Oh? Who's that then?'

Festus nodded at Marcus. 'His mother. She was kidnapped into slavery two years ago. His father was killed and Marcus escaped, only to be taken by a gladiator trainer. All quite illegal, you understand. They were Roman citizens and our former employer takes a dim view of fellow citizens being treated this way. He wants Marcus's mother found and released. If the man responsible for it can be found and made to pay for his crime then so much the better.'

Andreas glanced at Marcus. 'That's tough. I'm sorry for your loss, boy. Sounds like you've had a hard time of it.'

Marcus nodded, fighting back the emotions that had been awoken by revisiting his past.

'Anyway, what can I do for you?' Andreas asked. 'You think I know where to find every slave in Greece?'

'No,' Marcus replied, clearing his throat as he suppressed his feelings. 'But you can help us find the man who destroyed my family. His name is Decimus. He was a magistrate in Stratos at the time, and he owned land in the Peloponnese. He's bald and has a limp.'

Andreas nodded and scratched his chin. 'Can't say I know the man. I've been to Stratos a few times and never come across him. But there is a Decimus who is a tax collector. He has the contract for most of the towns in this part of the province. He comes to Chalcis twice a year to oversee the process.'

Marcus leaned forward. 'When is that?'

The Greek clicked his tongue. 'You just missed him. He passed through the area a few days ago. Won't be seeing him again until the end of the year.'

Marcus let out a frustrated sigh and clenched his fists.

'Do you know anything else about Decimus?' Festus intervened.

'No.'

'All right then, we'd be grateful if you kept this all to yourself. Is there anyone else you know of who might give us some information?'

'Not here in Chalcis. But there's a big slave market at Stratos. There are plenty of traders passing through. If anyone can help you locate the boy's mother, then they'll be able to.'

Marcus felt his blood go cold as he recalled the slave market and the night when he and his mother had been visited by Decimus who had gloated over their suffering. His stomach knotted painfully and he renewed his vow to make Decimus suffer when the time came for his revenge. A simple death would be too good for the man.

'Stratos, then.' Festus broke into his bitter thoughts. 'That's where we're headed. We'll try the slave market like you suggest, and see if anyone has information. We'd better make plans for the night and set off early in the morning. We thank you, Andreas. For your help. And the drink.'

'You're welcome. And thank you for the lesson. I'll think twice before I step up to fight any strangers passing through Chalcis again.' He drained his cup and peered into the jug, frowning when he saw that it was empty. 'Then I'll leave you to discover what pleasures the port has to offer.'

He rose from the bench and belched loudly before turning to Marcus. 'Good luck, lad. I hope you find what you are looking for.'

Marcus nodded his thanks and the Greek turned away, heading down a narrow alley towards the sunlit street that led back into the heart of the town. When he was gone Festus shook his head.

'I think it will be harder to find our man than we thought.'

'But we must find Decimus!' Marcus said urgently. 'We need to find out exactly where he sent my mother.'

'We know she's somewhere in the Peloponnese,' Lupus intervened. 'At an estate owned by Decimus. Perhaps it would be better if we started there.'

'Lupus is right.' Festus nodded. 'It makes more sense.'

'No,' Marcus responded firmly. 'We stick to my plan. We find Decimus and force him to tell us where he is keeping my mother, then we rescue her.'

Lupus pursed his lips. 'Why bother with Decimus? We've got just as much chance of finding the estate as we have of finding him. More, in fact, since estates are not in the habit of travelling around, as Decimus seems to be.'

His attempt at lightening the mood fell flat and Lupus folded his hands together and puffed his cheeks. 'Just saying . . .'

There was a brief silence as they looked out to sea. In the distance, across the blue water dotted with the square sails of merchant ships and the smaller triangular sails of fishing boats, lay the northern coast of the Peloponnese. The region's mountains towered up, grey and daunting in the distance. Somewhere in that direction lay his mother, and Marcus found it hard to be heading in the opposite direction for the present. But he had to pick up Decimus's trail first if he was to be led directly to his mother, he told himself.

'We could spend months searching the Peloponnese,' Marcus said quietly. 'We can't afford to waste any time. If Decimus hears we've been snooping around estates in the area, then he'll have my mother killed to destroy the evidence of his crime. We need to be careful and take one step at a time. First, we track down Decimus. That's my decision.'

'Your decision?' Festus cocked an eyebrow. 'We're all in this together, Marcus.'

Marcus turned to face him as he replied firmly, 'Caesar sent you to help me. Both of you. So we'll stick with *my* plan.'

Festus and Lupus looked at him for a moment before Festus raised a hand and ran his fingers through his cropped hair.

'As you wish, Marcus. But I can't help feeling that this is all as much about finding Decimus as it is about finding your mother.'

'We need to find him first in order to find her, like I said.'

'Perhaps. But if I were you, Marcus, I'd search my heart and ask myself a question. Which is more important – revenge, or rescue?'

Festus did not wait for a response but stood up and stretched, then grimaced and gently rubbed his ribs where Andreas had struck him with the staff. 'We need to find a place for the night. Then get a good meal, a decent sleep and be up and on the road to Stratos at first light. We'll get some miles under our belts before it's too hot. Then rest until the afternoon before we continue. Come on, let's move.'

Lupus stood first, and then Marcus, after a brief hesitation. They picked up their packs and headed back down the hill into the town. Festus led the way, then Lupus, while Marcus brought up the rear. None of them talked and that suited Marcus. He was thinking about what Festus had said. Was he driven more by the desire for revenge on Decimus, than by the desire to save his mother?

No! he thought instinctively . . . But then, the more he considered it, the more the burden of all the suffering that he had endured came trickling into his mind. The loss of his home. His dog, Cerberus, who had died defending him. Titus, who had raised and loved him as his own son. Then there had been the pain and hardship of the gladiator school where he had been branded on the chest with the mark of its owner. He raised his spare hand to touch his tunic above the scar, recalling the sickening agony of the heated iron pressed into his flesh. After that had been the terror of the fight in the arena of the school against two wolves. And later the fight to the death with the Celtic

31

boy-gladiator Ferax in the Forum in Rome. All of which had scarred Marcus's young mind. And all because of Decimus.

Getting revenge on Decimus was the only way he could see to remove the burden of all he had suffered. Another boy might have been driven mad by what had happened, Marcus reflected. The only thing that kept him sane was the thought of saving his mother. But he could not do one thing without the other. Revenge and rescue. The bitter truth was that he needed them both.

4

'Is that him?'

Lupus raised his hand and pointed across the street as a figure emerged from the gate. Through the opening Marcus could just make out the large yard beyond and the bars of some of the holding cells, before the guard closed the gate and slid the bolt across. Marcus switched his gaze to the fat man who had come out of the small prison where the slaves were held before auctions. His mind went back to the time when he had been in a cart that had passed through those same gates. He and his mother had been huddled in the bottom of a cage, sitting on soiled straw. The auctioneer had come out to inspect them. He was the kind of man that made an impression for all the wrong reasons. Overweight, sweaty and cruel.

'Yes, that's him all right.'

Festus nodded. 'Then we need to prepare. Lupus, you follow him and find out where he lives. Then come and find us back at the inn. Understand?'

Lupus frowned. 'I'm not an idiot.'

'I know that. But you don't have anything to prove to me. I don't want any heroics.' He tapped the boy on the chest. 'Just play safe.'

'I know what I have to do.'

'Good.' Festus glanced up and saw that the auctioneer had turned the corner and was struggling to get round a woman carrying two large baskets from a yoke across her shoulders. 'Then get after him, before you lose sight of the man.'

Lupus dashed across the street, dodging a pile of donkey manure that had fallen from the back of a cart, and closed in on his quarry. Marcus watched him with a slight shake of the head.

'He's not used to this kind of work. I hope he doesn't give himself away. You should have let me do it.'

'Too much of a risk,' Festus replied. 'You recognized him quickly enough. Who is to say he couldn't do the same?'

'But there are slaves passing through his cells all the time. Hundreds, thousands maybe. I'm sure he wouldn't remember me.'

Festus pursed his lips. 'Maybe, but why take the risk? Lupus will do all right. He's smart, even if he's not much use in a fight. And that we need to remedy as soon as possible.'

'What do you mean?'

'It's time we taught our young friend that the sword is mightier than the pen.' Festus smiled. 'While we're tracking down your mother, and Decimus, we'll teach Lupus how to use a few weapons, and try to get him in shape. I've a feeling we'll need all the muscle we can get before this is over.'

Marcus raised his hands in despair. 'But . . . Lupus? Are you serious? Put a blade in his hands and he's likely to be more of a danger to us than anyone else.'

Festus turned to face him, hands on hips. 'You think Lupus was any less promising than you were before you started training at the gladiator school?'

Marcus thought for a moment and nodded. 'As a matter of fact, I do. I was raised on a farm and I worked it alongside Titus and the few slaves we had. Lupus has always been a scribe. I doubt he would have survived what I had to go through even before I reached the school.'

Festus sucked his cheek and nodded. 'Fair point. Still, we'll make the best of him that we can in the time. Better to have someone who knows how to use a sword at our side rather than not. I'm sure he can pick the basics up.'

35

'I hope you're right,' Marcus replied doubtfully.

'Let's pray we don't get ourselves into a situation where Lupus needs to draw a blade.'

'How likely is that?'

Festus stared at him a moment, then gestured for Marcus to follow as he turned and headed back down the street in the direction of the inn where they had taken a room.

The hours passed but there was no sign of Lupus. Marcus had been fretting as the afternoon had drawn on. He sat on the worn bedroll with his back to the cracked plaster of the wall and rested his chin on his knees as he tried not to fear what might have become of his friend. Opposite him Festus lay asleep, snoring gently. Marcus wondered how he could rest so easily. In the end he could bear it no longer and, rising quietly, left the small room. He closed the latch behind him and stepped into the small courtyard behind the inn. In the past the rooms the landlord rented out must have been used for stores, or even animal pens, Marcus thought. He could still detect the residual acrid smell of goats. The doors to some of the other rooms were open to allow what breeze there was to pass through from the opening high on the wall inside. The only other occupants of the courtyard were six men sitting in a shaded corner playing dice as they shared a large jar of wine.

Marcus wandered out of the courtyard into the street and looked both ways for any sign of Lupus, but there was little movement. It was a quiet neighbourhood on the fringe of Stratos, which was why Festus had picked it so they could avoid drawing attention to themselves. Most of the customers at the inn were passing through Stratos, heading north or south along the road that passed through the town. The kind of people among whom three travellers would be easily lost. He settled against the wall and waited for his friend to return. More hours passed and the shadows lengthened across the street. The men playing dice eventually finished the game and headed into the inn for supper, and Marcus was left with the distant sounds of urban life: the occasional cry of an infant, a snatch of conversation and the braying of a donkey.

At length, his anxiety got the better of him and he decided to wake Festus and tell him they should go and look for Lupus. As he slipped the latch and entered the room Marcus saw that his companion was already awake, sitting on his bedroll as he worked a sharpening stone up and down the edge of his sword. He paused and looked up at Marcus.

'He's not come back,' said Marcus. 'What are we going to do?'

'Do? Nothing.'

Marcus raised his eyebrows. 'Nothing? What if something has happened to him?'

'If that's the case, then what could we do about it?'

'Go and look for Lupus. What else?'

'I see, we go and look for him in the dark, in the streets of a town we don't know.' Festus continued sharpening his sword as he tutted. 'What good will that do? Be patient, Marcus. We just have to wait for him to return. Sit down and rest.'

Despite his concerns Marcus knew Festus was right. He forced himself to return to his bedroll and lie down. But he could not sleep. Instead he lay with his eyes open, staring at the rafters of the room. Every so often there was a soft scuttling noise as a rat scurried across one of the beams, the only sound to interrupt the rhythmic scrape of the stone grating along the edge of Festus's sword. Outside dusk closed in around Stratos and then night fell over the town. Unable to see his blade, Festus finally set it aside and there was silence for a moment before he spoke.

'Marcus.'

'Yes?'

'If we find Decimus, what are your plans?'

Marcus took a deep breath. 'I will kill him.'

'What if he has Thermon with him? And others? He is sure to be guarded.'

Marcus remembered the cold-blooded killer that Decimus used for his most dangerous tasks. It was Thermon and his men who had killed Titus and kidnapped Marcus and his mother.

'Makes no difference,' Marcus responded. 'One way or another, I'll find a way to get close enough to stick a blade in Decimus's heart. He'll see me and know that I have had my revenge.'

'And then what?' asked Festus. 'His guards will cut you down. You'll be killed.'

'I don't care.'

'No? Maybe not. But your mother will. She'll be left alone in the world. Grieving for you, and your father.'

She had been grieving for Marcus's real father for many years already, Marcus reflected. She had never forgotten Spartacus, and once Marcus had discovered the truth about his past, those moments in his childhood when he had seen her look at him and quietly weep suddenly made sense. With a stab of guilt he realized that if he acted as recklessly as he wanted, then he would only add to her misery. Marcus sighed in frustration.

'Listen to me, Marcus.' Festus spoke softly in the darkness.

Only his outline was dimly visible against the drab gloom of the plastered wall. 'Sometimes in this life, we must be prepared to take only those opportunities that are genuinely offered to us. We have to deny ourselves the goals we desire, however strong the urge. I should have tried to teach you that when I was training you for Caesar. But he only wanted you to be good with weapons.'

'It's not surprising. That's all I was to Caesar, a weapon. Little more than a tool for him to use.'

'That's true, I suppose,' Festus conceded. 'But he did admire you. There was something he saw in you that set you apart from others. That's what he told me. Something special . . .'

Not for the first time Marcus felt a tingle of icy fear trace its way down his spine. Nothing escaped the attention of his former master. Although he might not know the truth about his real father, Caesar had his suspicions that there was more to his past than Marcus had revealed to him.

'You are free now, Marcus,' Festus continued. 'Free to choose what you will do with your life. You do not have to be a slave to the desire for revenge. There is only death awaiting you if you choose to pursue Decimus. That would be a waste. Worse, a tragedy. I urge you to think again. Whatever Decimus has done to you and your family, your first duty is to rescue your mother. Then, if you still wish to hunt him down, I give you my word that I will do all in my power to help you.'

Marcus propped himself up on his elbow and stared at the outline of the man opposite him. 'You would do that for me? Why?'

There was a brief silence before Festus replied. 'We are comrades in arms. Caesar ordered me to help you. My mission will only be complete when you are satisfied it is all over. Only then. I will stand by you, Marcus. Come what may. To the very end.'

Before Marcus could try to respond, he heard the sound of footsteps running across the courtyard. A moment later the door opened and Lupus stood outlined in the door frame.

'I've found the auctioneer's home!'

5

Lupus's eyes were gleaming with excitement in the dim glow of the oil lamp that Festus lit on his return.

'I'm sorry it took so long, but Pindarus spent most of the afternoon at the bathhouse.'

'Pindarus?' Marcus interrupted.

'That's his name. I overheard one of his friends call him that. After he left the slave pens he went to the baths. I followed him inside. He met with some men and they talked business most of the time. I was close enough to overhear.'

'He didn't seem suspicious?'

'No, Marcus. I'm sure of it. He was too busy talking to notice me. I just kept to myself and looked down at the floor.'

'It was an unnecessary risk,' said Festus. 'I told you to follow him. That's all.'

'And that's what I did. But when he went into the bath-house I was afraid I might lose track of him. I thought it would be best to keep close enough to see him. That's how I was able to overhear what he and his friends were talking about.' Lupus leaned towards Festus. 'I heard him mention Decimus's name!'

'What?' Festus started. 'Are you certain?'

Lupus nodded. 'As far as I could make out it seems that Decimus is sending a man to the auction in three days' time to buy some slaves for his estate.'

Marcus and Festus exchanged a look of surprise before Marcus beamed with delight. 'The Gods favour us! Finally. We just have to wait for the man and then follow him when he leaves Stratos with the slaves that he's bought. He'll lead us straight to the place where my mother is being held.'

Festus thought a moment and frowned. 'It sounds too good to be true. But perhaps you're right. This is the work of prov-idence. Or it seems like it. But what if there's more than one estate? Decimus is a rich man. He's made a fortune since he went into business with Crassus. A man like Decimus may have more than one such property. We have to be certain we find the right one before we go charging in.'

Marcus felt his surge of hope begin to subside.

'What if we follow Decimus's man, then ambush him and force him to tell us if he knows where Marcus's mother is?' Lupus suggested.

'He won't be alone,' Festus mused. 'Decimus's agent is bound to have some men with him to guard the slaves he buys. It's too dangerous to take them on. It would be safer if we followed him back to the Peloponnese. Then we can spy on the estate and make enquiries among the local people to see if they know anything about your mother.'

'What if we don't find anything?'

'Then we find out if Decimus owns any other properties and scout those out as well.'

'It could take some time,' said Lupus.

There was a brief silence before Marcus spoke again. 'There's something else to consider. If Pindarus is a good businessman, then he should keep detailed records of every sale that goes through his auction house. While my mother and I were never officially sold, there might be some record of our being there, and where we were being sent on to before I escaped. What do you think, Festus?'

The bodyguard thought for a moment. 'It's risky, but worth a try. The question is, where would he keep such records? It's most likely he keeps everything at his business, in an office.

That's where we should look first. The trouble is the place is locked and kept under guard.'

'What if he keeps them in his home?' asked Marcus. 'If the slave pens are kept under guard then it might be better to search his house first.'

Festus considered the idea and nodded. 'Assuming we can get inside.' He turned to Lupus. 'What is his house like? How many doors off the streets are there?'

'Three,' Lupus answered. 'I checked. One at the front and a smaller one down a side alley, and then there's a yard at the back, where the slaves can come and go.'

'How many slaves did you count?'

Lupus thought a moment. 'Three in the yard.'

Festus stroked his jaw. 'It's likely that's where they will sleep. Pindarus and his family will be in the main house. If we wait until the middle of the night we might get over the wall and find his study, then see if any records are kept there. You and I will do the job, Marcus. Lupus will stay outside in the street to keep watch.'

'What for?' Lupus demanded. 'Why can't I come with you?'

'Because two will make less noise than three,' Festus said firmly. 'No arguments. Now I suggest we all get some rest. We'll need our wits about us later on.'

★

45

A waxing moon hung in a clear, starlit sky and cast a pale light over the slumbering town of Stratos. Three barefoot figures hugged the shadow of a wall as they crept along the street towards the house of Pindarus. Lupus was leading the way and he paused to point across the road at an imposing door set in a high wall. On either side were the locked shutters of shops rented out by the auctioneer.

'That's the one,' Lupus whispered. 'The house has two alleys running down each side.'

Marcus looked at the other houses and noted that the area was similar to the wealthier neighbourhoods of Rome where narrow passages divided many of the larger houses from each other. These would provide good cover for the three of them as they went about their mission.

Festus looked each way along the street but nothing moved, except for the dark shape of a cat boldly making its way down the middle of the road as if it owned the town. He gestured for the two boys to follow and they padded across the street, then ducked into the alley at the side of the house of Pindarus. The walls rose up one on each flank, two storeys high, but ahead Marcus could see they dropped down where the garden began. Festus stopped when he came to the lowest point in the wall and turned to the boys.

46

'I'll need a leg-up. Both of you, make a step.'

Marcus and Lupus intertwined their fingers and offered their hands up to Festus. He used Marcus first, trusting the tougher of the two to bear his weight most readily. Resting his hand on Marcus's back, he pushed himself up and quickly found Lupus's hand. Marcus grunted with the effort of bearing the man's weight but held him up.

'All right, lads,' Festus whispered. 'Lift me, nice and steady.'

Straining his muscles, Marcus braced his back against the wall for support. Beside him he could hear Lupus groaning lightly with the effort. Festus was right about him, Marcus reflected briefly. Lupus needed toughening up.

'I'm going to use your shoulders,' said Festus. 'Ready, Marcus?'

'Ready.'

He felt Festus's foot lighten as the bodyguard drew himself up to the tiles on top of the wall. Festus scrabbled for Marcus's shoulder and then thrust himself up. The sound of his heavy breathing and scuffling as he struggled astride the wall sounded deafening in the confined space of the alley and Marcus glanced anxiously in both directions, but there was no sign they had attracted any attention.

'Your turn, Marcus.'

He saw Festus reaching a hand down to him, and used Lupus

to step up against the wall. His fingers groped in the air and then he felt the man's powerful grip clamp round his wrist, and he clutched at Festus's forearm as the latter drew him up the side of the wall on to the tiles running along the top. Marcus felt his heart pounding in his chest, partly from the effort but mostly from the anxious excitement of the moment. Looking down into the garden, he saw a long arrangement of paths, neat flower beds and ornately clipped shrubs. The sound of water tinkling in a fountain came from the far end, close to the slave quarters at the very rear of the property. The main house itself was dark and silent.

'Come on,' Festus hissed as he swung his legs down and lowered himself cautiously behind a large bush from which a sweet scent rose into the cool night air. Marcus followed suit and eased himself down before dropping the last few feet and landing softly on the soil. Both of them waited a moment before Festus emerged on to the path beside the flower bed. Fortunately, it was paved rather than gravelled and they made almost no sound as they followed it up to the rear of the main house. An outdoor dining area stood to one side, in the Roman style with long, low stone couches on which cushions could be spread for the comfort of guests. Next to the dining area was a portico with a corridor leading into the darkened interior of the house.

'How are we going to see our way inside?' Marcus asked as loudly as he dared.

Festus pointed into the darkness. 'By the front door. I'll wager there's a lamp burning beside the shrine to the household Gods. We'll use that.'

Marcus followed him into the dark corridor. They proceeded slowly, feeling their way cautiously along the wall. Some twenty feet further on, the corridor opened out into the atrium and a small amount of moonlight shone through the opening above the shallow pool that collected the rainwater. A staircase led up to the second level of the house where the bedrooms were arranged round a landing overlooking the pool. A faint sound of snoring came from above. On the far side was another short length of corridor, at the end of which a wan yellow glow came from a tiny flame.

'I thought so,' Festus muttered. 'Wait here.'

He padded round the edge of the pool and returned a moment later with a small oil lamp. The wavering flame gave just enough light for them to make their way back down the corridor in the direction of the garden. Festus stopped outside the first door and eased it open. He leaned in and raised the lamp high enough to see the interior, then backed out. 'Just a storeroom.'

The door on the next room let out a dull creak from the hinges as Festus opened it and both of them froze, straining their ears for a few heartbeats. But no one stirred and Festus resumed, easing the door open very slowly, while Marcus winced at each creak of the hinges. When there was enough space to squeeze through, Festus entered the room. Marcus followed and saw by the dim glow of the lamp a desk and a wall covered in sectioned shelves that were piled with scrolls and waxed tablets.

'Looks promising,' Festus whispered. 'Let's get started.'

He set the lamp down on the desk and indicated the shelves. 'You start at that end and I'll begin with the other.'

'What exactly are we looking for?' Marcus asked.

'Anything with a reference to Decimus, Thermon, or any estate in the Peloponnese. Your name, and your mother's, of course.'

Marcus nodded and padded to the end of the shelves, taking down a small pile of documents, then returning to the desk to look through them. There were bills of sale, inventories of each week's auctions, a running record of expenses and commissions relating to each sale, and a daily log. Pindarus was clearly in the habit of recording his business affairs in detail and Marcus felt his spirits rise. Such a man would have made some reference to the events of two years ago. Marcus and Festus worked methodically and silently through the scrolls and slates, section by section, being careful to replace them as they had been found. It was a while before it dawned on Marcus that he had been reading through documents in date order. He paused and looked up at the shelves, counting back to where he had started.

'Of course!'

'Shhhh!' Festus hissed.

'Sorry.' Marcus pointed to the shelves. 'I've worked it out. Each shelf, starting from the top left, represents six months. Which means that the one we are looking for is . . .' Marcus counted the shelves silently and then pointed. 'It should be that one.'

He crossed to it from the desk and bent down to retrieve the documents. Placing them in the light of the lamp's flame he opened a scroll and pointed to the date. 'There. It's the same year, two months from the date we were kidnapped by Thermon's men.'

Festus replaced the documents he had been looking at and began to sift through those Marcus had brought to the table. They examined them eagerly and Marcus felt a rising sense of excitement as he wound his way through the scroll on which Pindarus had neatly completed his log at the end of each day. Then he stopped.

'Here it is . . . *Arrival of cart with six slaves; two Nubians (nameless), two boys from Lesbos (Archaelus and Demetrius), one woman (Livia), her son (Marcus). Placed in cell XIV for auction next day.*' Marcus looked up triumphantly.

'Read on,' Festus ordered. 'Does it say anything about Decimus?'

Marcus began to wind the scroll, then stopped and looked up quickly.

'What's the matter?'

'I heard something. Outside in the corridor.'

Festus turned towards the door as a shuffling noise came closer. Then the handle turned and the door swung inwards. Blocking the door frame was Pindarus, in a flimsy linen nightshirt, oil lamp in hand. His flabby jaw dropped in astonishment as he stared wide-eyed at the two figures poring over the documents on his desk.

Festus reacted first, throwing down the waxed slate he was examining as he snatched out his dagger and raced towards the door.

His movement broke the brief spell and Pindarus lurched backwards, screaming in a high-pitched voice. 'Help! Thieves! Murder!'

6

'Quiet, you fool!' Festus snapped as he chased after the auction-eer. Marcus dropped the scroll and raced after his friend. Outside in the corridor he saw Festus with the bulky outline of Pindarus a short distance in front as he rushed into the garden.

'Help! Help!'

Festus sprinted another few steps and launched himself at Pindarus. He landed on the man's back, knocking him forward. The auctioneer let out a cry of terror as he fell face first against an urn. There was an explosive grunt before he lay still, with Festus sprawled on top of him. Marcus rushed over as Festus rolled to the side and came up in a crouch, dagger held out to one side, ready for action. But there was no response from Pindarus. No more cries of alarm, not even a sound of breathing.

Marcus dropped down beside the auctioneer's head and saw in the moonlight that it was twisted at an awkward angle where it butted up against the base of a heavy stone urn in which a small conifer had been planted.

'Something's wrong with him. Help me turn him over, Festus.'

Between the two of them they managed to turn the fat man on to his back and his head lolled limply on the flagstones of the garden path. A small, dark dribble spilled out of one of his nostrils as he stared up at the moon. Marcus knelt down beside him and lowered his ear above the man's lips, but there was nothing. No sound and not the slightest movement of air. He shuffled down and pressed his ear over the soft flesh of the auctioneer's chest but could detect no heartbeat. Marcus looked up at Festus.

'I think he's dead.'

'Impossible.' Festus held up his dagger. There was only the dull metal gleam in the moonlight. No blood. 'I didn't touch him. I held the dagger out to the side.'

'It wasn't the blade.' Marcus gestured towards the urn. 'He hit his head on that.'

'Damn. Stupid fool shouldn't have run for it.'

'Master! Master!'

They both looked round towards the bottom of the garden. There was a figure moving there, then another, and behind them the glow as a third approached, a torch held aloft.

'Master?' The first figure hesitated as he caught sight of Marcus and Festus. 'Who's there?'

'Quick!' Festus hissed. 'We have to get out of here.'

They left the body and raced over to the flower bed where they had crossed the wall. Marcus threw his back against the wall and cupped his hands. Festus clambered up, roughly placing his hand on the crown of Marcus's head to thrust himself up. His foot pressed heavily on Marcus's shoulder as his fingers grappled for purchase on the top of the wall. At once he threw a leg over and lay along the wall, then reached down for Marcus.

'Thieves!' The voice from the bottom of the garden called out as he hurried forward, outlined by the glow of the torch of the man behind him. 'Robbery! Raise the alarm!'

'Come on, Marcus!' Festus urged.

'Wait!' Marcus looked back at the house. 'His record scroll . . . I must have it.'

'No! There's no time. Pindarus is dead. If you're caught in here with the body they'll charge you with murder. We must go. NOW!'

He thrust out his hand and Marcus reluctantly grasped it to

55

pull himself up on the wall, his toes scraping the plaster as he scrabbled for any grip that would help him over the top.

'Don't let them escape!' a voice cried out. 'They're getting away!'

Emboldened now, the men were rushing up the path and Marcus knew the body of their master would be discovered at any moment. Festus dropped down into the alley and Marcus quickly landed beside him.

'What's happened?' Lupus asked anxiously.

Festus shoved him towards the street. 'Later! We have to run. Go!'

They started up the alley, feet slapping on the stones. They had almost reached the street when a shrill cry cut through the peaceful night air. 'Murder! MURDER!'

They ran into the street as the glow of more torches loomed above the walls of the neighbouring houses. They had not gone more than a few paces when a door opened in the next house and a man stepped outside. He saw the three figures racing past.

'Stop! Oi, you lot! Stop!'

They ignored the command and ran on down the street towards the inn where they had rented a room.

'Stop them!' the man cried out as he gave chase. 'Murderers! Stop 'em!'

56

More people began to emerge and then fifty paces ahead Marcus saw a group of young men heading up the street, talking cheerfully. As the man behind called out again, they stopped and saw the three figures racing towards them.

'This way!' Festus pointed to an alley and dived into it. Marcus and Lupus followed as the party further down the street began to echo the cry of the man chasing them. The alley was narrow, barely more than a pace wide, and hardly any moonlight penetrated the darkness. Marcus prayed to the Gods that they did not stumble over anything and twist an ankle or tread on anything sharp. Festus turned left at the first junction and they ran on to the next, then took a right fork. Behind them they could clearly hear the pursuit being taken up by more of the townspeople.

At the next corner they stopped, chests heaving as they gasped for air.

'Which way . . . now?' Lupus gulped.

'I'm not sure,' Festus said. 'I've lost my bearings on the inn. But we can't stay here.'

Marcus thought hard, taking account of the direction they had originally come from and the diversions that Festus had taken. He stepped towards the opening to another alley. 'This way.'

Festus hesitated. 'How do you know?'

'Trust me and just follow!'

Marcus plunged into the gloom and trotted down the alley. It was relatively straight and when they reached a small square with a well he continued across it and into the street on the far side. Behind them the sound of their pursuers was starting to grow more distant and Marcus heaved a sigh of relief. He slowed his pace for a little longer and then eased into a walk. A moment later they stepped out into a street that all of them recognized. The inn was in sight a short distance to the left. With his heart still beating fast, Marcus tried to affect a casual air as he led his comrades towards the opening into the yard. Then he heard the sound of voices and laughter and paused.

'Keep going,' Festus insisted. 'We have to get off the street as soon as possible.'

They walked into the yard and Marcus saw a handful of men sitting on the ground where the dice game had been taking place earlier. They were in their cups and called out a slurred greeting as the three figures passed by.

'Come on, friendsh! Come 'n share a drink!'

'No, thank you,' Festus replied with forced levity. 'Been a long day. The boys and I need some sleep.'

'Shuit yerselves . . .'

Marcus lifted the latch on the door to their room and hurried inside, closing the door behind them. Lupus collapsed on his bedroll and gasped as he caught his breath. Marcus slumped opposite while Festus went back to the door and opened it a crack to look outside. When he was satisfied they had escaped their pursuers and that no one had raised the alarm, he shut the door and sat heavily. A thin shaft of moonlight pierced the window and washed their faces with a pale blue tint. Marcus could see the fear etched into Lupus's expression as his chest rose and fell. Festus puffed his cheeks and stared fixedly at the far wall.

'Do you think . . . we're safe?' asked Marcus.

Festus cracked his knuckles. 'For now . . . But we were seen.'

'It was dark. They couldn't have seen clearly enough to identify us.'

'But they did see a man and two boys. Pindarus is dead. They will be looking for the killers.'

'But we didn't kill him on purpose,' Marcus protested. 'It was an accident.'

'Do you really think that will make any difference? You heard them. Murder, they said. They won't be in any mood for an explanation. Besides, we were caught in his house. Where we had no good reason to be. They'll say we were robbing his house and killed him when he came across us. And who can blame them . . .'

Marcus was silent for a moment. 'Then what should we do? Lie low for a few days, until the auction?'

'No. It's too dangerous. We have to get out of Stratos. As soon as possible.'

Lupus gulped. 'You mean now? Right away?'

Festus shook his head. 'Not while there are people out on the streets looking for us. Besides the town gates are closed for the night. The only way out is over the wall. If we were caught trying to escape that way they would instantly connect us to Pindarus's death. We'll have to wait until morning when the gates are open, and leave like any other travellers. I just hope they won't be watching for us.'

'What will they do if they arrest us?' asked Lupus.

'What do you think they do to murderers?' Festus responded curtly. 'We'll be put to death.'

'Put to death . . .' Lupus muttered. 'Oh no . . . Oh no.'

'Try and rest,' said Festus. 'We must rise early and leave the town, to put as much distance as we can between us and this place.'

'But what about the auction?' asked Marcus. 'What about the man who's coming from Decimus's estate? If we miss him, then we'll lose this chance to find my mother.'

60

'I doubt there will be an auction. Not without an auctioneer. As for Decimus's man, well, there's not much we can do now. We'll have to find another way to locate the estate. I'm sorry, Marcus, but we don't have any choice. We can't afford to stay here and wait.'

'But where shall we go?' asked Lupus.

Festus considered their options briefly before he decided. 'Athens. Decimus is sure to have a house there, along with everyone else who needs to show his face at the governor's palace. Besides, it's a large enough city that we won't attract unwanted attention. I'm sure we can pick up Decimus's trail there. And we'll be far away from the hue and cry over the death of Pindarus.'

Marcus shook his head in anger and frustration. This should never have happened, he told himself. All they were trying to do was find some information. They had never intended any harm to befall the auctioneer. It was a bitter irony that he had returned to Greece as a freed person, only to be hunted down again. If they became fugitives it would make his ambition to find his mother ten times harder. If they were caught, and blamed for the death of Pindarus, then they would die, and any hope that his mother would once again be free would die with them.

7

Festus woke them before dawn so they could prepare their packs for the day's march. They had paid for their room in advance so there was no need to worry about disturbing the innkeeper to settle up. As soon as there was light enough, they left the room and crossed the courtyard to the street. A couple of the men from the previous evening had curled up in the corner of the yard, sleeping off their drink, and one of them stirred, raised his head to look at them and then slumped down again, burped and mumbled incoherently as he tried to get back to sleep.

Only a few of the townspeople had yet stirred and Festus made for the southern gate of Stratos. As they drew near to it he turned into an alley and led the two boys down it as far as the locked doorway in an arch outside a shop.

'We'll wait here.'

'Why wait?' asked Marcus. 'I thought you wanted to leave as soon as possible.'

'That's right. As soon as possible, when it's safe to do so. At the moment we stick out like a sore thumb. We'll wait until plenty of people are on the streets and we can blend in with the rest of the traffic passing through the gate.'

Lupus yawned. 'Well, why couldn't we have waited at the inn?'

'Because the moment the innkeeper hears that a man and two boys are being sought in connection with the death of Pindarus, he'll report us to the authorities. If we'd stayed in the room we'd have been caught like rats in a trap.'

Lupus shrugged as he looked at the trickle of sewage running down the middle of the dingy alley. 'As opposed to rats amid the crap.'

Festus stared at him then laughed. 'Good to see you still have a sense of humour. That's something you could do with, Marcus.'

'Really? Name one thing in my life to laugh about,' Marcus challenged him and then squatted down, trying to make himself comfortable while they waited for the streets to fill.

An hour passed and slowly the hubbub of the waking city filled the air as the sun rose above the horizon and bathed Stratos in a rosy glow. At length Festus nudged Marcus with the toe of his boot.

'Time to move. Up you get. You too, Lupus.'

They picked up their packs and headed back up the alley to emerge into the street. Where it had been almost empty an hour before, now it was thronged with people, handcarts and small wagons drawn by mules, and the din echoed off the walls of the buildings along the thoroughfare. They slipped in behind the covered wagon of a spice merchant and followed it in the direction of the southern gate. At first they made steady progress but then the wagon slowed to a halt. Festus motioned to them to be patient, but Marcus ducked his head round the side of the wagon and saw a queue leading to the gate, where several armed men were scrutinizing those leaving the town and searching the wagons and carts. He casually turned to his comrades and spoke in an undertone.

'They're looking for us.'

'What?' Festus had a quick look and when he faced the boys he could not conceal his anxiety. 'You're right, Marcus. We can't stay together. They'll be looking for three fugitives. We have to split up and leave Stratos one by one. It would be better if we use different gates as well. Lupus, you and I will leave by this road. I'll get ahead of the wagon and go first. If you see them stop me, then go back and wait a while before trying another way out.'

'What about me?' asked Marcus.

'You turn back. Take the north gate and head out a mile or so along the road before you cut round the town. Stay out of sight as far as you can. We'll meet up by that crossroads we passed a few miles down the road south of Stratos.' Festus paused and looked at each of the boys. 'Lads, we're all on our own for now. If any of us get caught then the others have to continue without them. Understand?'

Lupus nodded uncertainly and Marcus realized that he was afraid. In truth, so was Marcus, and not just for himself. He fixed Festus with a firm stare.

'Promise me one thing. If I don't get out, then swear that you will do all you can to find my mother and set her free.'

Festus nodded solemnly. 'I swear it by all the Gods.'

Marcus turned to Lupus. 'You too.'

'Me? What could I do, all by myself?'

'What you have to. I had to deal with that when I was first all alone. And I was younger than you.'

Lupus pursed his lips. 'I'll do my best, Marcus . . . I swear.'

Marcus clasped him by the forearm and did the same with Festus. 'I'll see you later. Both of you. The Gods go with you.'

'And with you, Marcus,' Festus replied.

Marcus turned abruptly and began to stride away up the

side of the street, along the queue building up. He did not look back, but turned his thoughts to his own escape. He must be calm and not attract attention. Yet he felt that people were looking at him suspiciously as he walked through the crowded streets. Then, as he passed a public fountain, he saw a notice pasted on the plinth, offering a reward for the capture of the murderers of Pindarus. He did not stop to read it, but slowed enough to pick up the details. Sure enough, the town's authorities were looking for a man and two boys, and there was even a brief description that he recognized as being of himself. Marcus felt an icy chill grip his spine and he increased his pace. How in Hades had they managed to get a description of him? It had been dark. No one could have made out any such details.

He was still pondering this as he passed by the entrance to the inn they had stayed at. He glanced towards the opening into the yard and saw one of the men who had been playing dice there the previous afternoon, leaning against one of the pillars either side of the entrance. The next instant their eyes met and the man instinctively nodded a greeting as one does at a person one recognizes, but does not immediately grasp why. Marcus did not respond but turned his face away, continuing to watch the man out of the corner of his eye. He saw the man frown slightly and ease himself away from the pillar as he watched Marcus walk by. He did not look back but continued down the street, forcing himself not to increase his pace.

'Hey!' a voice cried above the noise of the traffic in the street. Marcus did not respond.

'Hey, boy! . . . Hey there! Stop!'

This time Marcus increased his stride, all the time staring fixedly ahead. Inside his heart was pounding and his stomach churned with anxiety.

'I'm talking to you!' the man called out. People were turning towards him and Marcus knew he had to get away quickly. There was a crossroads a short distance further on and he turned off the street just as the man called out again, loud enough to carry over the sounds of the crowd.

'He's one of 'em! He was with the man and the other boy! He killed Pindarus!'

Marcus broke into a trot now that he was out of the man's line of sight, threading his way through the crowded thoroughfare, muttering apologies as he brushed past people. He saw an alley opening to his right and dodged into it, increasing his pace to a run as he pounded away from the man raising the alarm. There was nothing for it now but to make for the other gate as fast as he could before word reached the men guarding it that the fugitives were still in Stratos and had separated. He only hoped that Festus and Lupus had escaped through the south gate before it was too late.

There was no sound of pursuit but Marcus kept running, keeping parallel to the road that led to the gate. When he judged it was safe, he rejoined the street he had originally been following and saw the northern gate fifty paces ahead. But his heart sank as he saw more men, armed with spears, standing either side of the arch leading out through the wall. The traffic was still moving slowly as he joined the people shuffling forward. Every so often the officer in charge of the party stopped someone and questioned them, especially any men accompanied by one or more boys. Marcus tried to control his breathing and appear calm as he approached the gate. There were only a few people ahead of him when he heard a distant commotion from behind. He dared not turn.

'You! Yes, you boy. Over here!' The officer beckoned to him and Marcus swallowed nervously, then approached and stopped in front of the man. The Greek scrutinized him closely. 'Are you on your own?'

'Yes, sir.'

The officer's eyes narrowed slightly. 'You're not from these parts. Your accent is . . . Roman.'

'Yes, sir.'

'What's your name?'

Marcus thought quickly. 'Tiberius Rufinus, sir.'

'What are you doing in Stratos?'

'Just passing through, sir. I'm on my way to Dyrrachium, sir. My father's serving in the governor's staff there. He sent for me. I've come from Athens.'

Marcus could hear a voice now, demanding that the crowd clear the way.

'Athens, eh?' the officer mused. 'Well, young Rufinus, I'd watch yourself. They're nothing but a bunch of thieves in Athens. Thieves, and worse, philosophers. Nothing in this world so dishonest as a man who thinks for a living.' He laughed and waved Marcus on as he turned his attention to the next person in the queue.

'Let me through, I say!' The voice cried out again, closer this time. Marcus forced himself to walk unhurriedly up to the arch and into its shadow. The crunch of footsteps echoing off the stones on either side sounded unnaturally loud.

'Close the gate!' a voice called out.

'What?' the officer called back. 'On whose authority?'

'The magistrate! One of the killers has been seen. Not far from here. Close the gate now and we'll have him!'

Marcus stepped out into the sunlight and had only walked a few more paces before he heard a howl of protest from those who were still stuck inside the town. Then the hinges groaned in protest as the gates began to close. He continued a short distance before he dared look back, just as the gates thudded into place, barring the exit. Relief washed over him as he turned away to walk casually along the road leading north from Stratos.

As Festus had instructed he walked over a mile, to be safe, eventually stopping where the road passed through an olive plantation with terraces of trees that spread across the rolling hills on either side. He sat in the shade of a poplar tree and waited until there was no one in sight before leaving the road to work his way round the town towards the south. The countryside was dotted with small farms and their surrounding olive groves and strips of crops, and Marcus had to pick his way carefully to avoid being seen. Once he blundered into an angry man with two hunting dogs who threatened to unleash them if Marcus didn't get off his land at once.

It took the rest of the morning to make his way round the town and rejoin the road leading south towards Athens. By now the sun was high above and the air was hot and still, and Marcus was sweating freely. He took his canteen out of his pack for a few swigs of warm water before replacing the stopper and continuing on. A few miles south of Stratos the road passed into a forest of pine and cedar trees at the foot of a mountain and the air filled with the comforting fragrance of the pines. He was close to the crossroads now and Marcus increased his pace, keenly anticipating the reunion with his friends. He rounded a final corner and ahead lay the clearing where the two roads met.

There was no one there. Marcus felt his heart sink, fearing that Festus and Lupus had failed to escape. The thought of continuing his quest alone momentarily tipped him into a deep pit of despair before he angrily forced the thought aside. If that was what fate had in store for him then he would deal with it, like he had dealt with everything else since that terrible day when Thermon and his thugs had destroyed his peaceful home on Leucas.

There was still some chance that Festus would find a way to escape. Marcus had worked with him long enough to know just how tough and resourceful Caesar's bodyguard was. With a sigh, he crossed the clearing and sat down heavily beside the milestone to wait.

There was only a short pause before he heard a twig crack in the trees nearby and turned round in alarm, one hand reaching for the throwing knife in a concealed sheath near the top of his pack.

'Marcus?' a voice called out cautiously.

He relaxed and eased himself. 'Yes, Lupus, it's me. You can come out.'

A figure appeared from behind one of the trees and moved out into the dappled sunlight. 'It's so good to see you.' Lupus could not help smiling. 'I was starting to worry.'

'I got out just in time,' Marcus told him. 'What about you? Any problems?'

Lupus shook his head. 'I was afraid, but I tried to look calm and unconcerned like Festus. But all the time I thought they would see through me. Anyway –' his tone brightened – 'we're all here. Together again.'

Marcus looked round. 'Where's Festus?'

'He told me to wait here and look out for you. He said he needed to find something.'

'Find something?' Marcus frowned. 'What?'

'This!' Festus's voice called out and both boys turned to see him striding out of the forest. He held two hares up in one hand while a sling dangled from the other. 'Dinner! Now let's get off the road and find somewhere quiet to roast these beauties. I'm starving!'

8

'That's the sharp end,' said Marcus as he carefully handed the training sword to Lupus. 'You don't want to hold that.'

The other boy made a face. 'Oh, ha ha. Very funny. I'm not an idiot, thanks.'

'Just starting with the basics.' Marcus grinned and then his expression became serious. 'Try the grip and when you're happy that you are in control of the sword, give it a few swings to test the weight.'

He stood aside to give his friend some space in the small clearing where they had set up camp half a mile into the forest. Once the ground had been cleared of pine needles and a hearth made with stones piled round, Festus had taken out his tinder-box and started a fire to roast the hares after gutting and skinning them. Marcus had a keen edge to his appetite and savoured the meat. It was hard to remember how bleak things had looked just a few hours earlier. Now, with food in his belly and the conversation of his companions, his optimism had returned.

It was after they had eaten and rested that Festus suggested they start Lupus's training. They began with strengthening exercises, making the scribe hold a large rock as he performed squats. Then they made him raise the rock overhead, again and again, until at last Lupus dropped it and bent forward, hands resting on his knees as he gasped for breath.

'A good start,' said Festus. 'But you'll need to do that every day from now on. Dawn and dusk, until your muscles are toned. And then as often as necessary to stay that way. After you've had a breather, Marcus will introduce you to the sword.'

Now, as he watched his friend try out a few cuts and thrusts, Marcus could only wonder at Lupus's poor technique. Then he relented. It was not fair to pass judgement so easily. After all, Marcus had spent most of the last two years training to fight and only that had made fighting techniques second nature to him. Before that he had been no more aware of the art than Lupus. There had been no call for it in the peaceful farm where he grew up.

Recalling his childhood, Marcus felt a deep, wounding sense

of loss. He had been raised in a loving home, and ranged freely over the surrounding farm as he played sometimes with the children from the nearest village. At the end of the day he would return home, with Cerberus panting at his heels, and the smell of woodsmoke and food from the kitchen would waft across the small courtyard. Invariably Titus would be sitting on the small stone bench, greeting him with a smile on his craggy face as he ruffled his hair and asked what his little soldier had been up to that day. Then they would go in to eat and later, as night fell over the farm, Marcus would go to bed where his mother told him a story while lightly stroking his brow, and sometimes sang to him –

'Marcus!' Festus called from the side of the clearing where he sat, rubbing linseed oil into the Parthian bow he had taken out of his weapons pack. 'You can't leave him to wave the sword around like that forever. You're supposed to be teaching him. Not daydreaming.'

'Sorry.' Marcus stepped forward as Lupus lowered his wooden sword. His face was beaded with sweat and he was breathing hard.

'Heavier than . . . I thought.'

Marcus nodded. 'The training weapons are designed that way. Helps build muscle and confidence for when you move on to a real weapon. Right then, we'll start working on your technique. Let's go over here.'

He led Lupus to the trunk of a pine tree he had chosen earlier. There were no branches for the first eight feet of its height and the trunk was about the thickness of a man's torso.

'In gladiator school we practise against stakes. This will have to do. I want you to imagine that this is a man. Try and picture a face at the same height as yours. Think of it as a man desperate to kill you. But you have to kill him first. That means that you must strike hard and strike quickly. Understand?'

Lupus nodded and made to strike.

'Stop!' Marcus commanded. 'You wait until I give the word. I want you like this.'

He stood a sword's length away from the tree and lowered himself into a half-crouch with his weight distributed evenly over his boots. 'Keep balanced on the balls of your feet and your toes so you can move quickly in whichever direction you need to.'

Marcus demonstrated with a few springs to the side, as well as forward and back, each time returning to the same position in front of the trunk. Then he gestured to Lupus to give it a try. The scribe did his best but was not nearly as agile and swift as his friend. But Marcus nodded encouragingly and then took the training sword and lowered himself in front of the trunk, making ready to strike.

'There are three basic blows. The thrust, and then cut to the left and to the right.'

He sprang at the trunk and hit it in the centre, withdrew, attacked again, both sides with sharp cracks as the wooden weapon struck the bark. He repeated the moves and handed the sword back to Lupus.

'You try.'

Lupus settled himself into place and then tried to do as Marcus had shown him. The blows were roughly on target but did not land heavily and the sound of the impacts was merely a muffled thud.

'No!' Marcus snapped at him. 'That won't do. This isn't a bloody game, Lupus. You're learning how to fight for your life. A sword is not a toy. You can't break it. You must treat it like an extension of your arm. When you strike, you are the one making the blow and you'll throw all your weight behind it. If not, then you'll barely scratch your opponent. And he will kill you. Put down the sword.'

Lupus did as he was told and Marcus stood directly in front of him, in a crouch. He raised his right hand and placed his palm on Lupus's chest. 'This is what you are doing at the moment.'

He gave a firm shove and Lupus lurched back slightly and recovered.

'And this is what you need to do.' Marcus braced himself and punched his hand out, twisting slightly as he threw all his weight behind the blow. Lupus went flying back and thudded to the ground. He lay there a moment, gasping, and then struggled up on to his elbow and stared at Marcus with a hurt expression.

'What did you do that for?'

'To teach you a lesson,' Marcus replied sternly. 'If you don't strike properly in a fight then you will lose. You will die. Better to learn that here and now. Get up and have another go. This time strike the target like you mean it. That trunk is Decimus. Him or any other person that has ever given you cause to hate them. Hit it hard, with your whole body thrusting through the sword. Pick it up and get to work.'

Lupus rose to his feet and looked at Marcus with a flash of hurt pride and anger in his eyes. He reached down for the wooden sword and resumed his place in front of the tree.

'Begin!' Marcus ordered.

'Hah!' Lupus grunted as he stabbed forward and the point struck the tree loudly. He drew the blade back and hacked at the side with a sharp thwack. Then the other side, then another thrust, grunting each time with the effort.

'That's it.' Marcus nodded. 'Keep doing it just like that until I say stop.'

He watched a moment longer and then moved off to stand beside Festus who had been looking on.

'What do you think?' he asked quietly.

Festus was silent a moment before he replied. 'I think you would have made a formidable gladiator instructor, young Marcus. You might want to think about that when this is all over.'

Marcus shot him a surprised look. 'No. I'll never train a person to fight another to the death just to entertain a crowd. I swear it by all that's sacred.'

The earnestness with which he spoke seemed to amuse Festus and he chuckled and shook his head. 'A pity.'

Marcus did not think so. Inside his stomach churned as he recalled the terror that had gripped him each time he'd been called upon to fight for his life. No one should have to endure that just to amuse other people. No one. He felt disappointed in Festus for even suggesting that he might want to be a part of the dark world of the professional gladiators. And a slight doubt crept into his regard for the man. Over the last few months he had come to assume that Festus believed in the same things as he did. He reminded himself that Festus had been

Caesar's man long before Marcus knew him, so his first loyalty would always be to the Roman aristocrat. There was a fundamental difference in outlook between Festus and himself. One that could prove very dangerous if ever Festus discovered that Marcus was the son of Spartacus.

He drew a deep breath and forced himself to turn his thoughts to more immediate matters. 'I meant, what do you think of Lupus? Has he got the right stuff?'

Festus regarded the other boy as he ferociously attacked the tree trunk. 'It's too early to say. Keep him at it, and he might make himself useful one day. Work him hard until dusk, and then we can all rest, ready for the road tomorrow.'

He turned and began to stride off.

'Where are you going?' Marcus called.

'I've something of an appetite for those hares. I'm getting some more. Make sure you keep the fire going.'

Marcus watched him disappear into the trees and returned his attention to Lupus whose blows had begun to slacken.

'Keep at it! Use all your strength. You can rest when I tell you, and not before!'

Lupus tossed the slender bones of the hare aside and used the hem of his tunic to dab the grease from his mouth.

'That was delicious.' He smiled contentedly. 'Best thing I've eaten in months.'

He lay back on the ground and stared at the night sky, a pool of stars fringed by the trees surrounding the clearing. Every so often a brilliant red spark swirled up to join the cold, steady pinpricks of the stars before swiftly fading out. Around them the forest was pitch-black, but the occasional light crack of a snapping twig, or rustle of undergrowth, revealed the animals who were abroad under cover of darkness. At first Lupus had been nervous, thinking the noises to be the sounds of men stalking them. Born and raised in Rome, he had little experience of the natural world. But he was growing used to it, and starting to enjoy the experience. Even the shrilling of the cicadas no longer bothered him.

'I could learn to live like this,' he muttered happily.

Festus grunted, chewing slowly on a morsel of meat. When he swallowed he wagged a finger at the scribe. 'It makes a nice change right enough. But that's because summer is coming. You wouldn't want to be out here in the winter. Believe me.'

Marcus had already finished his meal and sat staring into the flames. He nodded as he recalled the winter that had just passed, and the cold of the Apennine mountains that had seeped into his bones. He shivered at the memory. But he could understand

Lupus's feeling. Sleeping under the stars on a warm night filled his soul with a tranquillity he had rarely known since being torn from his previous life.

'Anyway,' Festus continued, 'we can't stay here. Too close to Stratos. Word of Pindarus's death and the hunt for his killers will spread out. We have to stay ahead of that and then find a way of disappearing from view. We should be able to manage that in a city the size of Athens.'

'But we didn't kill him on purpose,' Lupus protested. 'We're not murderers.'

'That's not how it looks,' Marcus interrupted. 'It's hardly as if we were invited into his house. No one will believe it was an accident. The only thing we can do is make sure we are not caught.'

'He's right.' Festus nodded. 'We'll have to travel as far from Stratos as we can tomorrow. Better if we get some sleep. We'll need all our strength for the road.'

Lupus smiled. 'Sleep. Just what I want. Can't tell you how exhausted I am.'

He reached for his cloak and pulled it over his body, then curled up with his back to the fire. His breathing soon became deep and even. Marcus and Festus sat in silence for a while as the fire began to die down and cast a wavering glow across the trees round the clearing. At length Marcus sighed, then spoke quietly.

'I wonder how Caesar's campaign is going?'

Festus shrugged. 'It's early days. Last I heard he was dealing with some tribes from Helvetia who wanted to settle in Gaul. You can be sure he'll make short work of them.'

There was a certain bitterness to his tone that caught Marcus's ear. He thought quickly, and wondered if Festus resented being ordered to help him. Marcus cleared his throat. 'Do you wish he'd taken you with him?'

Festus took a deep breath. 'I suppose I do. Having served him loyally for so many years I thought I would always be at his side.'

'Do you mind being told to help me?'

The man looked sharply at Marcus. 'No. Not now. At first, perhaps. It may sound strange but I find this situation more . . . comfortable. Being with Caesar is like walking a narrow mountain path. The view may be impressive, but you miss your step and you will fall. Do you understand?'

Marcus considered these comments then nodded. 'Even though I came to admire him, there was something about him that always scared me. I never thought he saw me as a person. More of a useful tool.'

'Exactly. That's how it seems to me, now I am no longer with him and can see things more clearly. That said, if he had decided to take me with him I would have gone willingly.'

Marcus shuffled a little closer to the dying fire before he continued. 'How long have you been in his service?'

'Twenty years. I was fifteen when he bought me from a gladiator school. Caesar was a lot younger. Just starting out in politics. It was a dangerous time; he had powerful enemies even then.' Festus smiled thinly at Marcus. 'I was like you. He saw me fight in the arena and decided I had potential. I was taken to Rome to be trained as a bodyguard by my predecessor. A big Celt who was as swift and deadly as a cat despite his size.'

'Oh?' Marcus could not recall any mention of the man before and dared to probe a little further. 'What happened to him?'

'He went the same way that many do in our profession. He was killed in a street fight. That was when I was twenty. Caesar appointed me to replace him as head of his personal bodyguard. In time, I dare say you would have taken over from me.'

Marcus raised his eyebrows. He'd had no idea that was the fate intended for him. He had always seen his relationship with Caesar as something temporary – a stepping stone on his journey to save his mother.

'You still may replace me, once this is all over and we return to Rome,' Festus continued.

'I'm not going back to Rome,' Marcus replied quietly.

'No?' Now it was Festus's turn to look surprised. 'Why not?'

'It was always my plan to return home after I rescued my mother.'

'Home? That farm on Leucas you told me about?'

Marcus nodded.

Festus sighed. 'You'd best forget that, Marcus. You told me your father got into debt trying to make the farm pay its way, right? So the chances are it has been sold on. It's almost certain someone else owns the farm now. You can't go back there.'

'But it belongs to us,' Marcus protested angrily. 'It's our farm.'

'It was. It isn't now. That is the way of things.' Festus tried to sound gentle. 'You cannot return to the past, lad. The Gods have decided on a different destiny.'

'No. I will return to my home. With my mother. I will find a way. I swear it.'

Festus smiled sadly. 'Very well then, Marcus. But one step at a time. First we must reach Athens and discover where Decimus is, and the estate where your mother is held. I had hoped we could find him without using official channels. There's a risk someone might warn him of our presence if we do that. But it can't be helped now. Get some sleep. There's a long road ahead of us.'

Festus settled back, arms folded behind his head, and closed his eyes. Marcus sat up a while longer, staring into the red glow of the embers, his heart filled with longing for home. The word conjured up so many feelings in his heart, with memories of all he valued most in the world. All the things that had been taken from him. The very thought of home had been a lifeline to him amid the raging storm of his life these last two years. The idea that there was no longer a home to return to filled him with anger and despair.

It was a long time before the seething emotions began to subside. The fire had died out long before Marcus finally lay down, huddled beneath his cloak, to fall into a troubled sleep.

9

They left the forest before first light and took the road south, leading away from Stratos. They walked fast, keeping a watch on the way ahead and leaving the road every time they saw other travellers. They bypassed every village they encountered so there would be no chance of anyone recalling that a man and two boys had passed through. The news of Pindarus's death and the reward for those held responsible for his murder would follow hot on the heels of Marcus and his companions, so it was essential to remain one step ahead of their pursuers until they reached the comparative safety of Athens, over two hundred miles away.

Once they had crossed the Achelos river Festus led them into the mountains of Aetolia, a largely uninhabited region where lonely shepherds tended the flocks of goats and sheep grazing on the slopes. There were very few villages, usually no more than a loose collection of stone huts, and they were forced to live off the land. Fortunately there were plenty of streams, gushing down rocky channels, and hares to hunt, as well as larger game. On the third day after fleeing Stratos, Marcus managed to bring down a small deer with his slingshot, the heavy missile knocking the animal cold before it even knew a human was nearby. They ate heartily that night and there was enough meat for two haunches to be put aside for the following days, with the burden shared between them.

They stuck to the mountains, passing Mount Parnassos where the snow still capping its lofty peak gleamed in the sunlight. That evening Festus decided they were sufficiently far from Stratos to risk stopping in the town of Delphi. Formerly one of the most important places in Greece, thanks to the Oracle in the temple of Apollo, Delphi had been visited by kings, generals and statesmen who sought to know their futures from the Oracle. The decline in the power of Greece and the rise of Rome had not treated the town kindly and Marcus noted the rundown nature of the streets after they entered the gate to find cheap accommodation for the night.

They took a dingy, airless room at the back of a small inn and wearily set down their packs as they surveyed their surroundings. The walls were cracked and stained and the large wooden frame of the only bed was covered with a torn mattress, from which grey, dusty straw poked out. Festus indicated the bed.

'You two share that. I'll sleep on the floor.'

Lupus made a face. 'I would have been more comfortable sleeping in the open.'

'Can't be helped,' Festus responded. 'There are too many farms surrounding Delphi. If we were caught sleeping on their land someone might ask difficult questions. This is safer. Now rest for a bit, then we'll go out to find something to eat when it's dark.'

'After that I want to look over the Temple of Apollo,' Lupus announced, his eyes gleaming with excitement.

Festus shook his head. 'Not a good idea. Let's just eat and turn in. We still have three more days on the road, at least, before we reach Athens. Besides, we shouldn't draw attention to ourselves.'

'But we're far away from Stratos,' Lupus replied. 'We're safe here. Surely? And plenty of people will be visiting the temple. We won't attract any attention. Come on, Marcus, what do you say?'

Marcus thought about it. He understood why Festus was

concerned. But perhaps the bodyguard was being overcautious. In any case, he had heard about the famous Oracle when living on Leucas and was curious to see the temple for himself. He turned to Festus.

'I don't see that there's much risk in having a look.'

Festus sighed with frustration. 'All right then. But stay close-lipped, and if I say we head back here, then there'll be no arguments. Is that understood?'

The boys nodded and Festus shook his head. He sat down, propping his head against his pack and closing his eyes as he muttered, 'I pray to the Gods that nothing bad will come of this.'

The meal, a stew of goat and herbs, was nowhere near as satisfying as the meals they had cooked for themselves in the mountains, but it was filling. They paid the bill and left the inn, one of many small establishments lining the square opposite the entrance to the temple precinct. With Lupus leading, the three of them passed between the columns and tall studded gates to make their way inside the wall that separated the sacred ground from the outside world. A paved courtyard stretched round the temple, illuminated by several large braziers fed with bundles of wood by junior officials of the temple in plain white tunics.

The three visitors looked up in awe as they slowly approached the steps leading to the door. Above them, the pediment carried a painted relief of the God Apollo driving a gilded chariot that shone fiery red in the glow of the braziers. On closer inspection Marcus decided that the whole precinct had a rundown appearance. Much of the faded ochre paint on the columns was peeling. The gold that had once flowed into the hands of those running the temple had all but dried up.

'Magnificent, isn't it?' Lupus commented.

Festus shrugged. 'Big. Yes. Seen better back in Rome. At least our temples and shrines are looked after properly.'

'But they are only copies of the Greek originals,' Lupus replied with a touch of irritation. 'So much of what we have was inspired by the Greeks. An amazing civilization.'

'If they were so amazing, I wonder how they became part of our empire and not the other way round,' Festus answered drily.

Lupus ignored him as he craned his neck to inspect the relief of Apollo. Marcus followed his example briefly, then lowered his gaze to look around the precinct. A handful of other people stood admiring the temple, while a wizened priest sat on the steps behind a small altar. He looked bored, but soon stood when he saw Marcus and his companions draw closer to the temple.

'Good evening, sirs. Care to make a donation to the upkeep of the temple?' He rattled a small wooden box. His voice dropped and his eyes narrowed beneath their bushy brows as he stared at them. 'Or, for a more generous payment, you could be given a glimpse of your future . . .'

Festus shook his head and laughed. 'Away with you! We'll not be taken in by your racket.'

'Racket?' The priest frowned, then drew himself up to his full height, some inches shorter than Festus, and touched his spare hand to his breast. 'Sir, do you dare to scorn the Oracle, here on the very ground that was sanctified by the God Apollo?'

Lupus nudged Festus in the ribs. 'Thought we weren't trying to draw any attention to ourselves . . .?'

Festus muttered a curse, then bowed his head in apology. 'I am sorry. I am a weary traveller. I spoke without thought.'

'Then you are forgiven, my boy.' The priest made a gesture with his hand, then held out the box again. 'And I'm sure a little something extra would go some way to appeasing Apollo.'

As Festus growled and reached for his purse Marcus took a step towards the priest, a strange gleam in his eyes. 'Wait, you said you could see into the future.'

The priest tutted. 'That's what we do here, as I am sure you're aware. For a small fee.'

Marcus stared back at him. 'How much?'

'The great men who have come here to know their destiny paid great sums for the privilege. But for ordinary mortals a lesser sum is acceptable.'

'How much?' Marcus asked again, impatient with the old priest. 'To tell me my future. How much?'

The priest eyed the three visitors shrewdly and tilted his head slightly to one side. 'You are clearly Romans of modest means. But Apollo takes an interest in all mortals for a small sum. Shall we say . . . five denarii?'

'What?' Festus's eyebrows rose in shock. 'FIVE denarii! Are you mad?'

The priest pointed a gnarled finger. 'I've already warned you. Do I call the temple guards to throw you out?'

'Pay him,' Marcus said firmly.

Festus turned to look at him in astonishment. 'It's too much, Marcus.'

'There's something I must know,' Marcus countered. 'The money was entrusted to me as well by . . . by our former master. Please, Festus, pay him.'

Marcus stared at the bodyguard intently for a moment before

the latter shook his head and took out five silver coins from his purse. He hesitated a moment before slapping them down on the altar. 'There. I hope it's worth it.'

The priest hastily scraped the coins into his palm, then raised one to bite on it with his remaining teeth. He held it up and squinted before nodding and feeding the coins into the slot on top of his box. Closing his eyes, he raised his face towards the night sky and his lips moved silently.

'Well?' Festus demanded.

'Shhh!' The priest's brow furrowed. 'I was just beseeching divine Apollo to accept your humble offering. Do not tax his patience any further, Roman, if you want him to look kindly on this boy's desire to know his fate.'

Festus glanced at Marcus and raised his eyebrows. Marcus was not put off by his cynicism but watched the priest closely, hoping fervently that the God of the temple would take pity on him and tell him the one thing he needed to know more than anything else: would he succeed in rescuing his mother?

The priest cocked an ear, as if listening, then nodded and bowed his head before he opened his eyes and turned to Marcus.

'Mighty Apollo deigns to answer your request, my boy. Quite a privilege.' He shot a quick look of annoyance at Festus. 'Despite the bad manners of your companion. A word

94

of warning, though. If the Oracle replies, it may be that the answer is not clear at first. But if you think it through, then you will know the meaning of the words. Now, follow me.'

He turned and started stiffly making his way up the steps with Marcus a few paces behind him.

'Oi!' Festus called out, indicating himself and Lupus. 'What about us?'

The priest glanced back. 'Yes, yes. You too. Might as well. But keep your mouths shut and show some respect.'

At the top of the stairs he led them through the columns towards the large doors of the inner sanctum. A brazier stood on either side, casting an eerie glow over the columns that towered up on either side. The priest paused in front of the doors and reached to the side for a brass-capped stick. He solemnly struck the door three times and cleared his throat.

'Oh, mighty Apollo! Is your mouthpiece, the blessed Pythia, prepared to offer guidance to he who would know his destiny?'

There was a pause and then a voice spoke, loud and deep, as if echoing from the back of a great cave.

'Come!'

The doors began to move, and there was a rumbling groan from the iron hinges. Marcus felt his pulse quicken as he looked past the priest into the darkness at the heart of the temple. He strained his eyes but could pick out nothing beyond the doors, save the flagstones nearest the entrance. The priest entered, gesturing to Marcus and the others to follow him inside. Their footsteps echoed off the walls rising invisibly around them. Marcus could see no sign of the person who had called on them to enter. The dim form of the priest stopped and struggled down on to his knees. Marcus and the others waited a short distance behind him.

'Philetus, who would speak to me?' A voice spoke softly from the darkness. A woman's voice, yet it was dry, and Marcus could not decide if it was an old woman, or young.

The priest turned and waved Marcus forward with a whisper. 'Go on, boy. Slowly. And stretch your arms out in front of you.'

'Wait,' Lupus hissed. 'Is it safe?'

Marcus smiled briefly at his friend. 'I'll know soon enough.'

He took a calming breath and raised his arms as instructed, then stepped forward cautiously. As he proceeded into the darkness, his eyes and ears strained to pick out any sign of movement. Then he heard it, a soft breathing, like the faint rasp of leaves disturbed by the gentlest of breezes. He slowed down and stopped as he became aware of a dark shape ahead. Then he felt his hands being taken and nearly jumped. But he resisted the impulse to snatch them back. A musty odour filled his nostrils. The hands were cold and the skin leathery. Fingers softly stroked the back of his hands while the other person's thumbs firmly applied pressure to his palms in order to hold them in place.

There was a long intake of breath before the voice came again. Louder now and more commanding. 'I am Pythia. Servant of the Oracle. Ask me your question, and if it pleases him, Apollo will reply through me . . .'

Marcus swallowed nervously and tried to sound calm as he spoke, but was conscious that his voice betrayed his age as well as his anxiety. 'My name is Marcus. I am on a quest to find and rescue my mother. I wish to know if I will succeed.'

There was a brief silence before Pythia replied in a rasping rhyme:

> '*A boy of great heart, torn from his home,*
> *No father, no mother, no hope has he,*
> *Cursed by the Gods for years to roam.*
> *At the end of his journey shall he be*
> *Bathed in blood and grief and hate;*
> *A terrible price to be paid for such a fate . . .*'

Marcus frowned. 'What does that mean? Will I save my mother? Tell me!'

'Poor boy,' Pythia replied with a hint of pity. 'It is for you to discern the meaning of the Gods. I only convey their message.'

'That's not enough,' Marcus said desperately. 'I need to know! Tell me!'

He grasped her hands tightly. The woman tried to pull her hands free but Marcus clung on, bracing his boots.

'Let me go,' the woman hissed. 'I command you to let me go.'

'Not until you tell me.'

'Sacrilege! Release me, before you anger the Gods!'

'Tell me,' Marcus pleaded. 'What does it mean? Bathed in blood?'

Suddenly she stopped struggling and stood still before him. Then she whispered. 'Blood . . . Blood . . . Blood everywhere. A land bathed in blood and fire. An eagle brought down, broken and maimed. I see . . . I see a man astride the eagle, sword in hand. Your father . . . Your true father . . . He sees you. He sees you! He calls to you . . .'

Marcus felt his blood chill in his veins and a terrifying icy sensation rippled up his spine and through his scalp as he listened.

'You . . .' she continued, her voice low and husky. Even though he could not see the woman Marcus sensed her eyes boring into him. That, and her terror. Her voice suddenly rose to a high pitch. 'You are the destroyer! I see death and devastation surrounding you!'

With a sudden powerful wrench, the woman snatched her hands free and Marcus heard her feet slapping across the floor as she hurried away into the darkness. Her voice wailed one last time. 'Flee! Death has come to Rome!'

Marcus felt a hand grab his shoulder and the priest spoke harshly in his ear. 'Get out! Go! Leave the shrine!'

Despite his age, the priest swung Marcus round and thrust him towards the open doors of the temple. He could see Lupus and Festus outlined by the glow of the braziers outside as the priest shouted.

'Be gone!'

Marcus backed away, then turned and hurried towards the door. His companions fell into step beside him as the priest repeated the command. They had barely left the inner sanctum when the doors closed behind them with a grating thud. They dashed down the stairs and did not stop as the servants of the temple and the remaining visitors stared at them. Outside, in the square, Festus led them down the first street they came to and they hurried on in darkness until they were a safe distance from the temple. Only then did Festus allow them to stop. Marcus leaned against a wall, gasping for breath as his shaken nerves began to recover.

'Well, that was great,' Festus panted. 'So much for not drawing attention to ourselves.'

10

'What do you think it means?' asked Lupus once they had returned to the safety of their room. 'All that stuff about blood, and a destroyer.'

He turned and looked at Marcus strangely as Festus left the room for a taper to light the single oil lamp, fixed in a wall bracket. Lupus lowered his voice. 'She must have meant Spartacus. Your true father!'

Marcus nodded, still dazed by the unnerving experience.

'That's it,' Lupus continued excitedly. 'She saw it all. The rebellion, everything . . . But at the end, when she said you were the destroyer, what was that about?'

Marcus did not reply. He couldn't. He did not fully understand it himself. He had already decided not to take up the legacy of his father. Not when it promised more suffering and another defeat by Rome's legions. Maybe, if there was a real chance of success, then one day Marcus might think about it. Now, he was still trying to puzzle through the meaning of the brief verse the woman had spoken.

'Marcus. If this is a message from the Gods, then it seems you are chosen to take up the cause of Spartacus. You will lead the slaves and crush Rome.'

Marcus rounded on his friend. 'Shut your mouth! Do you want everyone to hear you? You know my secret. Only you and a handful of others. That is how it must stay. Understand?' He grasped Lupus's tunic and yanked him closer so their faces were almost touching. 'You will not breathe a word of this to anyone.'

'Wh-whatever you say.' Lupus tried to shrink back but could not escape Marcus's grip. Marcus glared at him. In the dim light coming through the open door from the fire in the inn's dirty courtyard, he could see the fear in his friend's eyes. Ashamed, he released Lupus and took a step back.

'Sorry. I didn't mean to frighten you.'

Lupus patted his rumpled tunic back into place. 'That's all right, you don't have to apologize. I understand the danger you are in. But what about Festus?'

'What about him?'

'He heard what I heard.'

'But he doesn't know the truth about my father.'

'But what about that mark on your shoulder? The brand of Spartacus. He's seen that.'

'Yes,' Marcus nodded. 'But he does not know what it means.'

'No,' Lupus conceded. 'But he might be suspicious after what the Oracle said.'

Marcus pursed his lips. Lupus was right. Festus would try and work out what lay behind her words. If he guessed the truth then Marcus had no idea how he would react. He heard the sound of footsteps approaching and shot an urgent look at Lupus.

'Not a word. I can't afford Festus to know the truth.'

Lupus nodded as the bodyguard appeared in the door frame, cupping a hand round the small flame at the end of a taper. He ignored the boys and held the flame to the wick of the oil lamp until it was alight. Then he puffed his cheeks and blew on the taper to extinguish it before closing the door.

'There. That's better.'

Marcus and Lupus sat on the bed while Festus remained standing, arms crossed as he regarded Marcus. He was silent for a moment and Marcus could feel his heart beating anxiously as Festus cleared his throat.

'That was . . . unexpected. I knew the Greeks had a passion

for drama and theatrical effects, but that was a better show than any you'll see in Rome.'

Marcus cocked an eyebrow. 'Show?'

'Of course. The deep voice was probably someone speaking down a large voice trumpet. The doors were opened and closed by servants in the shadows on either side and I liked the touch of the woman in the darkness. All very theatrical, don't you think?'

Marcus and Lupus glanced at each other before Marcus nodded. 'I suppose.'

'Oh, come on, lads! You weren't taken in by that nonsense. Surely?'

Marcus felt embarrassed. Had he been fooled? Or was there more to it than Festus saw?

'They've been conning visitors to the temple for hundreds of years. Putting on a bit of a show and giving out mumbo-jumbo verses. The trick is to make it all sufficiently vague that the mark can read just about anything into the prophecy they are presented with. I've seen enough fortune-tellers on the streets of Rome to know how it works. They prey on the gullible. The big temple, the stage effects and so on may be more impressive here in Delphi, but it's still the same old game.'

Marcus felt himself flush with shame. What Festus said made

sense, and he had seen the same fortune-tellers and knew that his companion spoke the truth. Yet he could not explain how the woman in the temple had known so much about him. And he had not sensed any acting in the dread that gripped her at the end. She had tried to free herself, pulling her hands back powerfully. But for the strength gained from his gladiator training, Marcus could not have restrained her. And the terror in her voice had been real. No, he decided. She had seen something, had a vision of some kind. She had known what he was, the son of the leader of the great slave rebellion. If that much was true, there must also be some truth in her verse.

'And now we're poorer by five denarii, thanks to Marcus,' Festus continued. He reached down and patted his purse. 'We've got less than a hundred left. If we continue to put on our fights we can make it last a few more months. But if we haven't found your mother in that time, then we'll have to return to Rome.'

'No,' Marcus responded firmly. 'I will not leave Greece until I have found her. I swear it on my life.'

Festus eased himself down on to his haunches so that his face was level with Marcus. He smiled sadly.

'Marcus, I will do all I can to help you find her. But you should also prepare yourself for the worst. We may never find her. She may not even be alive. If that's true then you need to be ready to deal with it.'

'She's alive!'

'That's what we must believe, for now. But it is wise to prepare yourself if she is not. You will need to make a life of your own.'

'Then I will deal with that, when I have to. But for now I believe she is alive, and waiting for me to find her. And I will.'

Festus stared at him then stood up again. 'All right. We'll do all that we can to save her. First we must find Decimus and that estate of his. Let's concentrate on that. We'll reach Athens in a few more days and find some answers there. Now, it's been an exciting evening. Let's get to sleep.'

He turned to the bedroll he had made from their spare clothes and his cloak, easing himself down. Lupus and Marcus took off their boots and belts to lie down on each side of the bed, hearing it creak under the burden of their combined weight. Marcus turned his back to Lupus and stared at the wall.

'Shall I put out the lamp?' Lupus asked.

'No,' Marcus cut in before Festus could respond. After the unnerving experience in the temple he could not bear the thought of darkness again. At least not that night. 'Leave it burning.'

'As you wish.' Lupus turned away and began to breathe easily. Soon a telltale throaty click indicated that the scribe was asleep. Marcus rolled gently on to his back and crossed his arms behind his head. There would be little sleep for him tonight. The words of the Oracle went round and round his mind.

> *At the end of his journey shall he be*
> *Bathed in blood and grief and hate;*
> *A terrible price to be paid for such a fate . . .*

What did it mean. Whose blood? Why the grief and hate? What was the terrible price he must pay? A sense of foreboding crept over him. Would his single-minded hunt for his mother lead them into danger? Would he be responsible for the death of either, or both, of his companions? Or was his own life the price that must be paid? Or, far worse, would it be his mother's life?

He heard Festus stir and clear his throat softly.

'Marcus, you should try to sleep.'

'I can't.'

'That prophecy has really got to you, hasn't it?'

Marcus did not reply immediately. 'Are you surprised?'

'I'm surprised, no – disappointed, that you have let it bother you so much. All that rubbish about blood, fire and your father. I'm sure Titus was a good soldier, but from what you've told me, he doesn't sound like a man of destiny.'

'No. I suppose he doesn't. Not Titus.' Marcus felt a shiver of concern. He should have called Titus father, and not referred to him by name. Praying that Festus had not picked up on it, he raised his head and risked a glimpse at the bodyguard. Festus lay on his side, propped on an elbow to stare straight at him.

'Marcus, you and I have served Caesar together long enough for us to trust each other. With our lives, but also with the truth.'

Marcus felt the familiar tingle of anxiety at the nape of his neck.

'Is there a secret you are keeping from me? Maybe there was something in what the Oracle said. Why else would you react so? What is it, Marcus?'

Marcus chewed his lip and tried to think quickly. 'I trust you with my life, and you are my friend and comrade in arms . . .'

'But?'

Marcus swallowed nervously. Now he must lie and make it sound convincing. He had no choice. If he told the truth Caesar's bodyguard might hand him over to the authorities at the first opportunity.

'I have told you where I came from, and about my family. You know the truth about me. The whole truth.'

'And I have your word on that?'

'Yes.' Marcus forced the word out.

'Then there's nothing more to be said. Now get to sleep, Marcus.'

Festus lowered himself and lay flat on his back, shutting his eyes and breathing deeply until he began to snore. Marcus listened with envy, wishing he could put aside his worries and sleep as easily as his older comrade.

His thoughts returned to the words of the Oracle. She had said that his father, Spartacus, had called out to him, that he was the destroyer, and death had come to Rome. Was this the destiny that Brixus had urged him to embrace? It had been a while since the former gladiator who had fought at his father's side had entered his mind. Marcus recalled how forcefully Brixus had urged him to become the figurehead of a new slave revolt. This time, Brixus promised, they would succeed where Spartacus had failed. Once word that his son was leading the rebellion spread out, runaway slaves would flock to his banner and create such a host as Rome had never seen. This time the legions would be overwhelmed and crushed by sheer weight of numbers, and the scourge of slavery would be lifted from the world that had languished too long in the shadow of the eagle emblem of Rome.

But Marcus had seen that such promises were mere dreams. Brixus had too few men to start a revolt, and Rome would react swiftly and cruelly to any new attempt by slaves to overthrow their masters. The time was not right. Marcus had refused to cooperate with Brixus and the veteran gladiator had been outraged.

Yet now he had been offered a vision of the future, one depicting the death of Rome. Perhaps Marcus was being offered a second chance to continue the work of his father. But it sounded a fearful prospect and Marcus was not convinced he should expose the world to the terrible images conjured up by the Oracle. He needed someone he could talk to about his dilemma; keeping it all to himself was intolerable. Only his mother would understand and offer him the comfort and advice that he sought – one more reason to devote himself to rescuing her.

A soft moan of despair caught in his throat and Marcus clenched his eyes shut, struggling to drive all thought from his mind so that he could get the rest he so desperately craved.

11

They continued on the road to Athens. Sleeping in a cheap inn at Coronea the first night, Marcus resumed training Lupus in the morning and evening while the scribe grumbled about his aching muscles. But the atmosphere had changed between them. Cheerful conversations were now less frequent and they trudged on, each wrapped up in his own thoughts.

As promised, Lupus did not raise the subject of the Oracle's prophecy again, but that did not stop his searching glances at Marcus, most of which the latter noticed but pretended to ignore. Festus led from the front, seldom looking back at the others as he strode on, setting a fast pace. Only when they stopped for a rest, or to refill their canteens from a mountain stream, did he enter into any exchange. But now Marcus saw a suspicious glint in the man's eye every time he looked at him. Marcus still felt shame over his deception as well as fear that he would have to guard against Festus in the days to come.

Late in the afternoon on the day after leaving Coronea they came to the modest town of Leuctra. A local religious festival was taking place and all the cheap inns were full. The only rooms left were in a far more expensive inn on the town square and Festus gritted his teeth in frustration as he broke the news.

'There's nothing for it. We'll have to spend another night in the open.'

Lupus looked up at the sky. Clouds had been rolling over the mountains during the afternoon and threatened rain. 'I had hoped we'd be sheltered tonight.'

'Can't be helped,' Festus replied tersely. 'Better we go now and see what we can find in the country close to the town.'

Marcus intervened. 'Or we could place a little wager on ourselves and win enough to cover the accommodation for tonight. What do you think?'

Festus was about to refuse when a distant rumble of thunder echoed off the surrounding mountains. He looked around the town square and saw that although many of the stalls had packed up for the day there were still plenty of people about.

He weighed up their options then nodded to Marcus. 'All right. Same drill as before. Let's get to it.' They moved to the base of a statue of Hermes that dominated the square and removed their cloaks, then took out the training weapons from their packs. Lupus stood over the possessions, a thick stave in his hands.

While Marcus stood back a step, Festus raised his hands and began his patter. 'My friends, hear me! Good people of Leuctra I am honoured to visit your famous town. No doubt there are many men here who are descended from the great warriors who served noble Leuctra in the wars against Persia . . .'

As Festus continued, Marcus surveyed the crowd and saw the usual bands of youths, as well as a group of thuggish-looking men at a table outside a wine shop. There would be no problem finding contenders among these people, he decided. The men at the wine shop turned to hear Festus.

When Festus issued his challenge, their leader, sitting at the end of the table, made a comment and his cronies burst into laughter. He was a powerfully built man with a shock of dark hair and he wore studded leather bracers. Easing himself on to his feet, the man gestured for his gang to follow and approached the small crowd in front of Festus. Four of the local youths had already volunteered and had moved to take up the wooden weapons. The man and his surly-looking followers pushed their way through the crowd.

'Put those down,' he ordered the youths.

One of them, a tall, well-built teenager, turned round with an angry expression, fists clenched. But as soon as he saw who had spoken he quailed and Marcus saw his Adam's apple bobbing nervously as he stammered.

'Sorry, Pr-Procrustes. I didn't know it was y-you.'

'Well, now you do, you and your boys can shove off.'

'Y-yes. Of course.' The youth turned to his companions. 'Let's be off, b-boys.'

They hurriedly dropped the training swords and withdrew into the crowd. Caesar's bodyguard flashed a polite smile at the man called Procrustes.

'I take it that you are stepping forward to challenge myself and the boy, sir?'

The Greek glared back. 'No. I'm stepping forward to put the boot in, Roman. You don't come into my town and play your games without asking for my say-so first. That's how it works in Leuctra.'

'I apologize most humbly.' Festus bowed his head. 'I was unaware of the protocol.'

'Protocol?' Procrustes laughed harshly. 'Hear that, boys?

We've got a proper Roman gentleman among us today. Well, Roman, I'll tell you what. You leave me your baggage and your purse and get out of Leuctra at once, and I'll let you off the beating I usually hand out to those who don't abide by the correct, er, protocol.'

Marcus could see Festus's fingers twitch slightly, a telltale sign that he expected violence to explode at any moment. He glanced at Lupus and nodded discreetly towards Festus's pack as he whispered, 'Arm yourself.'

Festus continued smiling as he addressed the Greek. 'And if I refuse to hand over all our worldly goods? What then?'

'Then me and my boys will give you a hiding you'll never forget.'

'I see.' Festus looked him up and down. 'I take it you are the local crime lord.'

'That's a nice way of putting it. But I see myself as more of an extra-legal businessman.'

Festus forced a quick laugh. 'You have a ready wit. That is good. But do you have a ready eye for a fight, sir? As I am not prepared to give up our belongings, let me make you an offer. You and three of your men take on me and my lad, Marcus, here. If you win, you take our stake: ten, say twenty, denarii. If we win, you pay us the same.'

Procrustes thrust out a muscular arm and poked Festus in the chest. 'I will not be insulted by such an easy challenge. I shall take on you alone. And to make it interesting I'll take your wager. But let's fight for a man's stake. If you lose, you lose everything you have, including those two.' He nodded towards Lupus and Marcus. 'They'll fetch a decent price at the slave market in Athens. If you beat me, and you won't, then I'll pay you a hundred denarii. Leaving aside the boys, that's worth more than twice the value of your kit. What do you say?'

'And if I refuse?'

'Don't refuse,' Procrustes said in a low menacing voice. 'Not if you want to live to see another day.'

'Then what choice do I have?'

'None. And there's one other thing. It's just you and me. The boys stay out of it. I want them in good condition once I've seen to you.'

Festus considered this for a moment and then nodded. He handed the Greek a wooden sword. 'Better get your friends to clear some space.'

While Procrustes bellowed the order to his gang, Festus approached Marcus and Lupus and spoke in an urgent under-tone as he thrust his purse into Marcus's hand. 'If I lose, get out of here as fast as you can. Run and don't stop for anything. Then make for Athens. The governor there should help you.'

Marcus shook his head. 'We stay with you. Let's leave the town. All three of us.'

'I can't, Marcus. We make a run for it now, we'll not get far in the crowd. This way, there's a chance.'

Marcus looked at Procrustes as the latter swung his sword to test its weight and balance. 'He knows what he's doing. This won't be like the usual fights.'

Festus chose a training sword and followed the direction of Marcus's gaze. It was clear from the way that he carried himself and the ease with which he wielded the double-weight weapon that the gang leader was a seasoned fighter.

'He's been in the arena,' Marcus decided. 'That, or he's been a soldier at some time.'

'Then at least he'll put up a decent fight for the crowd and present me with a genuine test of my skills,' Festus said calmly. 'Something that's been sorely lacking in the towns we've passed through, so far.'

He turned back to Marcus and Lupus. 'Remember what I said, boys. If I lose, make yourselves scarce. Immediately. Understand?'

Lupus nodded but Marcus did not respond. Festus gripped his arm tightly.

'Think of your mother. If you don't do as I say, then you'll never see her again.'

The thought filled Marcus with pain, but there was no real choice between his comrade and his mother. He nodded.

'Good. Then wish me luck and pray to Fortuna!'

Festus turned and stepped into the open space cleared by Procrustes' men, keeping his face to his opponent and easing himself into a balanced crouch. Procrustes took up his position and rolled his head round to loosen his neck. The Greek gave an evil grin, exposing his teeth and revealing gaps that Marcus guessed were caused by fights. His neck, such as it was, seemed to merge head and shoulders seamlessly and his chest was like a barrel. Beneath the hem of his tunic his massive thighs balanced on calves as sturdy as the legs of a vast table. His forearms were like hams and he swung the sword in an easy ellipse in front of him as he called out to the crowd.

'People of Leuctra, I will give you a show this evening. And a lesson. This is what happens to those who choose to confront Procrustes. Leuctra is my town. Mine. I will crush anyone who forgets that. Now let's begin the lesson, shall we?'

He strode towards Festus and then slowed as he came within

two sword lengths. Marcus saw them size each other up, then Festus stepped forward and extended his arm, touching the end of his training sword against that of his opponent. Procrustes held his weapon firmly and then, with an easy twist of his forearm, he thrust Festus's sword away. Caesar's bodyguard came on without hesitation and feinted and stabbed at the Greek, but Procrustes easily blocked each thrust with a speed and dexterity that, while not graceful, was perfectly effective and demonstrated an excellent technique. Marcus knew that his comrade would need every ounce of his skill and experience. 'Your friend is a fool,' a voice hissed close by and Marcus turned to see a middle-aged lady swathed in a black cloak. There were streaks of grey in her dark hair and her eyes appeared sunken. 'Procrustes will break every bone in his body before the fight is over.'

'How do you know?'

She turned to him with a piercing gaze and her lips trembled. 'Because that's what the monster did to my son when he refused to pay protection money on his market stall. He died a few days later.'

Marcus was silent for a moment before he responded softly. 'I'm sorry.'

'Save your grief for your friend.'

Marcus turned back to the fight. 'Festus can handle himself well enough.'

'Then, if there's any justice, he will humiliate Procrustes.'

Festus fell back a few paces to open a gap between them and the Greek gang leader sneered. 'Had enough already? Then it's my turn.'

He stepped forward in a slight crouch, well poised on his feet, and made a swift series of feints and genuine thrusts at his Roman opponent. The sharp crack of wood on wood echoed around the square and the crowd, which had been silent, began to mutter and let out gasps as Festus easily defended himself.

'Come on, Procrustes!' one of his thugs bellowed. 'Beat his brains out!'

The Greek paused and called back. 'When I'm ready. I want to play with the scum first.'

Lupus cupped a hand to his mouth and cried out. 'Get him, Festus! I know you can do it!'

Those in the crowd looked at him in surprise and the woman nudged Marcus. 'I'd shut that young man up if I were you. If you want to save him a hiding once Procrustes has defeated your friend.'

Marcus took a deep breath and shouted. 'Go on, Festus! Cut him down to size!'

'Your funeral,' said the woman.

Procrustes went forward again, mixing a few brutal cuts into his attacks. Festus nimbly dodged aside to parry the blows away and the Greek drew back again, breathing heavily.

'You're good, Roman. I'll give you that. Best I've fought in a while. You're fast with a blade, but there's no real strength there.'

Festus smiled thinly. 'Think so? Then maybe you're in for a surprise.'

He leapt forward and struck out at the Greek's head. Procrustes instinctively threw up his sword arm to block the blow. Then Festus turned his blade and sent it down. Instantly, Marcus knew he had timed it too early and Procrustes punched his arm out to parry the redirected blow. Then, incredibly, Festus flipped his wrist again and the flat of the sword smacked into the side of the Greek's head.

The crowd let out a cry of surprise as Procrustes staggered back, desperately warding off more attacks, training swords clattering against each other as they moved across the open space. Festus landed another blow, on the gang leader's left wrist, and he let out a roar of pain and anger as he snatched his arm back.

'Hit him again, Roman!' the lady cried shrilly, waving her bony fist. Her cry was taken up by a few others in the crowd,

121

and the thugs backing Procrustes craned their necks to see who was defying their leader. No doubt they would take their revenge later on, Marcus thought. If their man won.

Festus pressed home his advantage, his training sword moving with blistering speed as it danced round his opponent's weapon. More blows landed and Procrustes gave ground, falling back towards his gang members as he desperately defended himself. More and more of the crowd were daring to cheer Festus on now and Marcus felt his hopes rise as he joined in, punching his fist into the air.

A fresh attack by the Roman drove Procrustes into the ranks of his followers and Festus stepped forward to finish him off. He never saw the blow coming. Marcus did, but before he could shout a warning it was too late. One of the thugs bunched his fists up, braced his boots against the flagstones and powered into Festus's side, unleashing a torrent of punches to his chest and head. Festus staggered back in a daze as the crowd shouted angrily. But the incident had given Procrustes a chance to recover the initiative and he charged forward again, hammering away at the Roman's sword.

Marcus was filled with outrage at the intervention and now his anger turned to dread as he saw Festus shuffle away from his enemy, head rolling as he struggled to recover. Procrustes struck out and gave a roar of triumph as the point of the wooden sword stabbed into the Roman's thigh, just above his knee. Festus's expression twisted in agony. At once the Greek struck again, smashing the training sword out of the other man's hand, and it clattered to the ground some twenty feet away, leaving Festus helpless.

Procrustes' supporters let out a roar and punched their fists up as they shouted his name over and over. The Greek stretched up to his full height and spat with contempt at his opponent.

'Let's finish this lesson the old-fashioned way!' he called out, grasping his sword in both hands as he raised his knee and placed it behind the blade. With a sudden, powerful movement the wood shattered and splinters flew through the air. The gang leader tossed the ends aside and raised his fists.

'Marcus!' He looked round as Lupus plucked his tunic. The scribe jerked his head towards the nearest street leading out of the square. 'We have to go. Now!'

He was still for a moment, then looked back and saw Festus feebly raising his fists to defend himself. Whatever happened he did not feel he could abandon his comrade. Marcus pulled himself free of Lupus's grasp. 'No.'

'But he told us to go if he lost. We have to run, while we can still get away.'

'Festus hasn't lost,' Marcus replied defiantly. 'Not yet.'

'Marcus, don't be a fool. Let's go.'

'I'm staying to the end.'

'Suit yourself,' Lupus snapped and turned to ease his way out of the crowd. Marcus felt torn between following his friend and staying, but he could not bear the sense of betrayal that coiled in the pit of his stomach.

In the open space, Procrustes steadily advanced on his Roman opponent, his fists inscribing small circles in the air. Festus shook his head to clear it and clumsily raised his own fists. The odds did not look promising, Marcus conceded. The Greek was at least half as big again as Festus, and his punches would carry great force behind them. Proscrustes shot his right fist out and Festus desperately knocked it to one side before raising his hands to protect his head. Procrustes steadily unleashed a series of jabs, probing his opponent, and although only a handful got through, Marcus winced each time his friend's head snapped back. Then the Greek stepped up the pace, trying to pummel the Roman's chest. Again some blows got through and Festus staggered back gasping as blood ran down his face from a cut above his right eyebrow.

'Ha!' Procrustes reared up, fists held out and high as he prepared to claim victory. He turned slowly so the crowd could clearly see him. Although his gang members were cheering at the top of their voices, the rest of the crowd's support was muted, though none dared support his challenger any more.

Marcus gritted his teeth. 'Don't give in, Festus! Don't give in.'

As if in answer to his urging, the bodyguard drew a deep breath and stretched up. He strode towards Procrustes. At the last moment one of the thugs called out a warning and the Greek began to turn round – just in time to take a blow to the jaw. Festus followed up with his left, and then the right again, an uppercut this time that sent the gang leader's head snapping back. He weathered a few more blows before recovering his stance ready to renew the fight. But Festus had no intention of getting into a slugging match. Stepping forward he drew his right arm back as if to punch his opponent in the face. Instinctively the Greek raised his fists to block the blow. That was when Festus swung his boot in instead; a vicious blow right on the other man's kneecap. Procrustes bellowed in agony and staggered back as Festus kicked again, into his groin. The Greek doubled over and received a knee in his face, and more blows to each side of his head as Festus swung his fists as hard as he could.

'Come on, Festus!'

Marcus turned and saw that Lupus was back.

'Thought you'd gone?'

The scribe shrugged and gave Marcus a sheepish grin before he continued shouting support for their comrade.

The crowd erupted in cheers and the woman beside Marcus screamed shrilly as she urged him to finish the gang leader off.

'Kill him! Break his neck!'

Festus leaned down and raised his opponent's chin with his left hand. The Greek swayed as his eyes blinked wildly. Festus bunched his right fist and drew it back as far as he could before unleashing a powerful blow from the shoulder that carried his whole weight behind it. Procrustes flew backwards and crashed heavily to the ground. Festus stepped over him, breathing deeply as blood dripped on to his unconscious opponent. Marcus grabbed Lupus's sleeve and pulled him forward. They ran over to Festus as the crowd began to roar with delight. The members of the Greek's gang looked round uncertainly, some with fearful expressions as the mob celebrated the fall of Procrustes.

'Are you all right?' Lupus asked anxiously.

Sweat ran from Festus's brow and his chest heaved. The cut above his eye was beginning to swell. He licked his lip and spat out some blood before he cocked an eyebrow at the scribe. 'Just great. Next stupid question?'

He breathed in deeply and winced as he clutched a hand to

his side. 'I need to go somewhere to rest and recover . . . Sweet Jupiter, that brute has a punch like a sledgehammer! But he's been cut down to size now. Before we go I'll take what's ours.'

Festus leaned over Procrustes and removed the purse from his belt. Beneath the soft leather it felt light enough to contain only a handful of coins.

'That'll do us, boys. Now let's get out of here.' He nodded towards the thugs who were starting to shuffle across the open space. 'They don't look very forgiving. Let's go.'

With Marcus and Lupus supporting Festus, they returned to their packs and picked them up. The woman who had spoken to Marcus earlier was grinning like a maniac and planted a kiss on Festus's cheek before she hurried away into the crowd. Other townspeople shouted their congratulations and patted him on the back as the three of them worked through the crowd towards the rear of the square. Suddenly a flash of lightning bathed the town in a brilliant white glare. A moment later thunder crashed from the heavens and the rain began to fall – a few drops rattling off the roof tiles at first, then in earnest as silver rods slashed down on Leuctra.

'We have to find shelter,' said Marcus.

Festus shook his head. 'Not here. Not in the town. Outside.'

'What?' Lupus turned to look at him with a surprised

expression. 'I thought that's what the fight was about. So we could afford a decent room?'

'That was before our friend back there decided to use the situation to cement his hold over the town. He won't be out for long. We shouldn't be around when he regains consciousness. Something tells me he's a sore loser. We have to get out of Leuctra. Before Procrustes recovers and comes looking for us . . .'

12

It rained hard for over an hour before the storm had passed. In that time Marcus and the others had left the town and made their way two miles down the road towards Athens before Marcus announced his decision to get off the road. His breathing was laboured and every few paces he grimaced and clutched a hand to his chest. It was dusk and the sun had already set by the time the clouds began to clear, leaving a golden hue across the western horizon. They stood next to an abandoned, roofless building beside the road. A faded sign on the wall revealed it had once been a wayside inn.

'Why?' Lupus asked, shivering as he stood in his drenched tunic and cloak. 'Surely we should just put as much distance between us and Leuctra as possible.'

Marcus shook his head. 'We're not going very fast. If

Procrustes comes after us you can bet he'll be moving faster. If they catch up with us on the road . . .'

'He's right,' said Festus. 'We have to get off the road and find somewhere to rest. I can't go on . . . much further without a . . . rest.'

They saw a path a short distance away and turned on to it, following it up a small hill into some olive groves. On the far side the path continued uphill towards a forest of cedars and poplars, passing over an open meadow. In the failing light they saw a herd of goats clustered round a handful of pine trees. Marcus glanced across the slope and could just make out the dim outline of a young goatherd resting against one of the trunks. Then they entered the forest. After a hundred paces or so there was a natural clearing round a jumble of rocks and Festus halted them.

'This will have to do. I can't go any further.' He sat down heavily and rested his back against a boulder.

'Want me to light a fire?' asked Lupus as he lowered his pack.

'No,' Marcus answered. 'What if anyone sees the glow? The last thing we want is for those thugs to find us.'

'That's not entirely true,' Festus intervened. 'I've been think-ing it . . . through. If I was Procrustes, I'd want my money back, and I'd want . . . revenge on those who had humiliated him in front of the people of . . . Leuctra. So we can be sure he will come. How far he will follow is anyone's guess. If he picks up our trail and finds us here we'll need to prepare. And we'll . . . light a fire to lure him in.'

Marcus sucked in a deep breath. 'That's madness. You saw his men. Big brutes, and there must have been nine or ten of 'em. We can't take on that many. Not with you in poor shape and Lupus barely able to handle a sword.'

Lupus shot him an irritated look. 'Thanks.'

'Then we must make a few preparations to improve the odds in our favour. Listen . . .'

While Lupus prepared a fire Marcus set to work cutting lengths of wood from the surrounding trees, passing the bundles of wood to Festus for sharpening. As the night fell they worked faster, knowing it was likely their pursuers would track them down before too long. Under Festus's instructions Marcus and Lupus surrounded the clearing with traps to ambush Procrustes and his men, should they make an appearance during the night. Then, when they were done, Lupus built up the fire and they settled down to wait.

'Lupus, you take the first watch. Give it two hours, as best you can judge it, and then wake Marcus so he can take over. I'll take the last watch.'

131

Marcus looked at him anxiously. 'How are you feeling now?'

'Like I've been run down by a herd of elephants. It's going to hurt like blazes tomorrow . Now let's rest. Lupus, keep your eyes and ears open for any sign of danger. We can't afford to let them catch us unawares.'

Lupus nodded. 'You can rely on me.'

It was past midnight and Procrustes and most of his men were sitting down a short distance from the goats. They had been searching for the three interlopers who had caused such damage to his reputation among the people of Leuctra. The cheers they had given the Roman after he had knocked Procrustes to the ground still rang in his ears and he burned with humiliation and anger. Pain was something he had long since grown used to, and his bruises did not bother him as he thirsted for revenge. No one, but no one, got the better of Procrustes and lived to tell the tale.

Once he had recovered from his beating, the gang leader summoned his best six men and set off after the Roman and the two boys. It had been easy enough to discover they had left the town and taken the Athens road. The gang followed it for five miles before reaching a small village with an inn where a few customers were still drinking. They had seen no sign of the travellers Procrustes was after, so he turned back and explored the first half-mile or so of every path that led off the road. Just as his men began to tire of searching, muttering and grumbling among themselves, they came across the goats and the young boy who looked after them. Terrified to find himself surrounded by several large men in the depths of the night, he tried to make a run for it. He never made it out of the ring and was placed in front of Procrustes, his arms pinned behind his back.

'Hold still, you little wretch,' he growled. 'Or I'll tell my man to rip your arms off.'

The boy ceased struggling at once.

'That's better.' Procrustes tried to soften his tone. 'We ain't going to hurt you. Not if you help us. But if you don't do exactly what I say then someone's going to find your body with your head caved in. Do I make myself clear?'

The boy nodded vigorously.

'I can't hear you, lad. Now tell me, are you going to do what I want?'

'Y-yes, sir,' the boy whimpered.

'That's better. Now then, how long have you been resting here?'

'From late yesterday afternoon, sir.'

'Excellent. So then you'd remember if anyone came up this path since then.'

The boy nodded.

'Again, I can't hear you. Speak up.'

'Yes, sir.'

'Did you see anyone?'

'Yes, sir. Three of them. A man and two boys. Just as it was getting dark.'

'It's them all right!' One of the thugs chuckled.

Procrustes snapped his head round towards the man. 'Shut it, you!'

'Sorry, boss.'

He turned back to the boy. 'Where did they go?'

The goatherd pointed up the path towards the forest. 'In the trees. And that's where they still are, as far as I know.'

'How do you know?'

'I saw the glow of a fire a while back, sir. I was curious. I heard that brigands had been spotted in the mountains and wanted to make sure my flock was safe. I went up to look and saw the three of them sitting around. Then I returned to the flock.'

One of his gang members muttered, 'I don't see any glow.'

Procrustes sighed. 'That's because they've probably let the

fire die down, you fool. Anyway, I have to be sure they're still there. Don't want us all blundering through the trees and alerting them. You go. Take the boy with you. He can show you where he saw them. Then get back here and make your report. If they're still there, we'll surround 'em and give them a nasty surprise.'

That was a short while earlier and now Procrustes was sitting in silence, relishing the prospect of getting his revenge, thinking about the most painful and shameful agonies he could inflict on the Roman. Then they would retrieve the purse he had taken from Procrustes. After that, they would take the boys and their possessions and sell them at the market in Leuctra to make sure the townspeople understood the fate awaiting anyone who defied him.

A rattle of loose stones from the path broke into his reverie and he stood up as two shapes headed down the slope towards them – the boy and the man sent with him. The latter caught his breath before he made his report.

'Just like the lad said, boss. They're in a clearing, asleep round a fire. It's burned right down so there's not much light. But I could see 'em. All three of 'em. Asleep like innocent lambs.'

'Lambs to the slaughter.' Procrustes chuckled menacingly. 'Right then, let's get them.' He paused by the goatherd and ruffled his hair. 'Good job, lad. When you've got a few more years under your belt, come to Leuctra and look me up. Maybe I'll have a place for you in my gang.'

He led his men up the path towards the trees. When they reached the fringe of the forest he stopped and turned to them. 'I don't want any of them to get away. So we don't just pile in there. When we get close we'll spread out round the clearing and surround them. When I give the word, charge in and we'll wake the scum up. Make it nice and loud. Clear?'

The men nodded in silence and he waved them on. 'Nice and quietly then.'

He led them slowly along the path, taking care not to tread on any fallen branches. Beneath the canopy of the trees it was almost completely dark and only the faintest of illumination from the stars penetrated the gloom to reveal the trees on either side. They had not gone far before Procrustes' eyes detected a faint glow between the trees ahead.

'Easy now, lads,' he whispered as he proceeded step by step.

As they drew closer the glow intensified, casting a red wash over the nearest trees and the boulders scattered across the clearing. Then he saw the bright glitter of a small flame as the fire came into view. In the dim light cast by the fire he saw a figure on the ground, covered in a blanket. Close by was a second. Both seemed to be asleep. Which left one other. Procrustes carefully scanned the surrounding area and then smiled as he saw the last of them, propped up against one of the boulders, also apparently asleep. If he was supposed to keep watch while his comrades slumbered, then he was betraying their trust. They would all pay the price for his failure. Procrustes turned back to his men and indicated for them to go right and left. While they crept off into the shadows their leader stayed on the path to keep watch over their intended victims. Every so often he heard the faint rustle of a disturbed branch and waited for the lookout to stir. But there was no sign that his men had been detected and it seemed the lookout was fast asleep. He waited until he was certain that the last of his men would be in position and then drew his sword, gritting his teeth as it scraped free of the scabbard. Holding it out in front of him, Procrustes stood and made his way along the track towards the fire. When he reached the edge of the clearing the trees gave way on either side of the rocks scattered across the ground. The nearest of the Romans was only twenty feet ahead, a dark form against the glow of the dying fire.

Drawing a deep breath, Procrustes readied his weapon, then bellowed at the top of his voice. 'Get 'em!'

His men took up the cry and surged in from the trees surrounding the clearing. As their leader raced up the path towards the fire he felt delirious with excitement that his plan was succeeding so well. Anticipating the satisfaction of killing Festus, he was just a few paces from the nearest of his victims when he heard one of his men cry out in pain. Then another, and he slowed his pace – but too late to stop himself stumbling into the concealed ditch that stretched across the path. A sharp, agonizing pain shot through his foot. With a deep groan, he plucked his foot out of the trench and stumbled on, consumed by his desire for revenge. More cries of surprise and pain came from the fringes of the clearing as he blundered on, right up to the nearest of the sleeping Romans, to deliver a vicious kick. The blanket slid to the ground, revealing a leather bag and some small pine branches carefully heaped in the shape of a reclining body.

Then Procrustes realized what he had led his men into. 'Get out, boys! It's a trap!'

Festus cupped a hand to his mouth as he stood up behind a rock at the edge of the clearing. 'Let 'em have it!'

Swinging his sling up, Marcus whirled it overhead as he picked a target. One of the men had charged by him so closely that Marcus had feared he would tread on him. But he had blundered past and was now clearly outlined against the fire just twenty paces away. Three other men had made it as far as the fire. The rest had fallen victim to the wooden spikes and other traps concealed about the clearing. Marcus took aim and released his shot. The heavy stone caught the man right between the shoulder blades. Stunned by the impact, he slumped forward on to his knees. Further round the clearing Marcus saw Lupus taking his shot. His aim was rushed and the missile struck his target on the forearm – a painful wound, but not crippling. Festus had drawn his sword and was charging down the path from the opposite end of the clearing. His blade tore into the stomach of the nearest gang member. With no clear target left, Marcus drew his own sword and charged towards the man who had kicked one of the dummies.

The man turned as he sensed Marcus's approach and he saw that it was Procrustes. The gang leader limped round and Marcus glimpsed the blood flowing from the wound in his foot where the Greek had impaled it on a spike. Then Marcus raised his sword and charged home, hacking at the man's head. Procrustes parried the blow and thrust Marcus to one side. Scrambling to a stop, he managed to keep his balance and turned back towards the gang leader.

'So, I must deal with one of the Roman's whelps before I cut down the man himself,' Procrustes sneered.

Marcus did not reply but came on in a crouch, sword point up and to the side, as he had been trained. The gang leader thrust at him, but Marcus saw the blow coming and swerved to the side, hacking down into his opponent's forearm before swivelling round and inside the reach of the man to thrust his blade up with as much strength as he could summon. It was a purely instinctive move, and he had made no conscious decision to kill the gang leader. Yet the point of the sword pierced Procrustes' throat, driving up through the skull into his brain. His face was close to Marcus, and his eyes were wide and staring as his head trembled uncontrollably. His jaw sagged as he muttered incoherently. Then his fingers released their hold on his sword and it thudded to the ground.

There was a hot rush of blood as Marcus wrenched the blade free and stepped back, shocked by the violence he had unleashed. Procrustes slumped to his knees with a horrible keening noise, then toppled over beside the fire, his stunned expression washed in the red glow of the embers as his blood pooled around him. Marcus stood over him, chest heaving, every muscle in his body tensed.

'Marcus,' Festus said gently.

He looked up and saw the bodyguard a short distance away, a concerned expression on his face.

'It's over,' Festus said. 'Lower your sword, boy.'

Marcus blinked as the battle rage began to drain from his body. He saw that he had instinctively raised the point of his blade towards his comrade, and lowered it and took a deep breath.

'All right now?' asked Festus.

'Yes. Fine. I'm fine.'

Festus looked down at Procrustes, whose body was twitching gently as the last of his life drained out of him. 'Pity. I had hoped to finish him myself. Three are dead, including him, and the rest are wounded. Good work, Marcus. And you, Lupus.'

Marcus saw his friend emerging from the gloom into the dim pool of light cast by the fire. He carried a sword and blood dripped from the end of the blade. Marcus saw that he was trembling. Around them he could still hear the cries and moans of the wounded.

'What now?'

Festus shrugged. 'We could finish them off. Or we let them live and send 'em back to Leuctra.' He paused and looked at Marcus. 'Your choice.'

Marcus was surprised. 'My choice. Why?'

'Because I think you are ready to make some of your own decisions. It's time to decide what kind of a man you will become.'

Marcus frowned. Why was Festus doing this? And why now? His mind was too tired to think clearly and he raised a hand to rub his brow as he considered the choice Festus had given him. It made sense to finish the gang off and bury the bodies. They would be discovered eventually, but hopefully by then Marcus would have found his mother and returned home. On the other hand, he was sickened by the bloodshed he had witnessed over the last two years and had no desire to add to it.

'We let them go.'

Festus searched his face for a moment and nodded.

'What about the dead?' asked Lupus. 'What do we do with their bodies?'

'Leave them where they are. If anyone cares about them, they'll come and find them. Not our problem.'

The four survivors from the gang were set free from the traps and their wounds dressed with cloth from the tunics of their dead comrades. One of them had been stabbed in the stomach by a concealed stake and was coughing up blood and moaning, supported by two of his companions. Marcus realized it was unlikely that he would live.

Festus stood in front of them, regarding them with contempt. 'So much for your attempt to murder us while we slept. Your leader is dead, along with two more of your gang. We could

142

have killed you all. But we're not murderers or cowards who strike in the night. So you get to live. But I want you to remember this. Go back to Leuctra and warn your friends what happened. Let them know that if we pass this way again and find the town still in the hands of your gang, then we'll complete the job we started tonight. Is that understood?'

The men stared at him, their fear evident in their expressions.

'I said, is that understood?' Festus repeated loudly. 'Or do I have to carve the message into your chests with my knife?'

The men nodded quickly.

'Then get out of my sight, before I change my mind. GO!'

They turned and stumbled down the forest path leading back to the road, the mortally injured man groaning in agony as his companions dragged him away. Marcus watched until they had disappeared into the darkness. Suddenly he felt utterly exhausted as the nervous energy drained from his body.

'You boys did well tonight,' said Festus. 'Now get some sleep. It'll be dawn in a few hours. I'll stand the last watch.'

Lupus nodded mutely and made his way back to the fire to retrieve his cloak that had been used to shroud one of the dummies. He settled down close to the embers but Marcus hung back beside Festus. The man turned to look at him.

'What is it?'

'Did I make the right choice?' Marcus asked.

'Only you can know that.'

Marcus sighed. 'But what would you have done?'

Festus thought briefly before he answered. 'I'd have killed them.'

'Oh . . . Then I made a mistake.'

'No. You did the right thing from your point of view. I'm different. Perhaps if you had lived as long as I have then you might have decided differently. There's no right or wrong in this, Marcus. Only a difference in perspective. Now get some rest. We've still got a full day on the road ahead of us when the sun rises.'

13

The road crested a ridge and there before them lay the great city of Athens, bathed in the afternoon sun. Lupus gazed down, eyes wide with excitement as he took in the details. Athens was dominated by the complex of temples and shrines surrounding the lofty columns of the Parthenon, constructed on the great rock of the Acropolis. Around it sprawled the markets, theatres and prestigious homes of the city's wealthiest citizens. The remains of the long wall that linked Athens to the port of Piraeus still stretched across the intervening countryside, but it was in a poor state of repair, neglected once the threat from Persia and the other Greek states had faded away. The scribe stepped on to a rock near the road for the best view and laughed with delight.

Marcus stopped beside the rock and looked up at him. 'What's the matter, Lupus? Never seen a Greek city before?'

'Not this one!' He beamed. 'I can't tell you how often I've dreamt of coming here one day. And now there it is . . . Athens!'

Festus joined them. The bruises resulting from the beating he took from Procrustes had come out in vivid reds and purples. Walking under the burden of his pack had added to his pain and he had been forced to slow his pace, letting the two boys lead. Now Festus eased his pack down and joined them as they gazed on the most famous of the Greek cities.

He was silent for a moment before he grunted, 'Not very big. I was expecting something more, given the way the Greeks go on about it. Not a patch on Rome, or Alexandria.'

'Size isn't everything,' Lupus said with a trace of irritation. 'Athens may not be the biggest city in the empire but it is the wisest.'

'Wise, eh?' Festus shrugged. 'A lot of good that did 'em.'

Lupus ignored his dismissive comment and turned back to gaze at the city. 'This is where the greatest philosophers come from. The greatest playwrights, sculptors and poets. This is where the very idea of democracy was born. Right there in the Agora.' Lupus pointed down at the marketplace, and the columned gardens that stood beside it. 'That's where Socrates, Plato and Aristotle taught their theories to their students.' Lupus's eyes blazed with a passion that Marcus had never seen in him before. 'How can you not be moved by the prospect of walking in their footsteps?'

'Right now, my feet are killing me,' Marcus groaned. 'I'd be more moved by the prospect of taking the weight off them.'

Lupus made a face. 'How can you not be excited?'

'Because we're here to find my mother. I don't care much for the rich history of the place. I just want to know where Decimus is, or his estate. That's all. Try to remember that.'

Lupus's expression changed. 'Of course. I'm sorry. Just got a bit carried away.'

Festus carefully stretched his back and winced. 'Now that we've had our little moment of cultural appreciation, would you mind if we got on? We still have a few miles to go.'

Lupus climbed down and grumbled as he bent to lift his pack and heave it on his shoulder once more. When all three were ready Festus gestured ahead and they started down the slope towards the distant city. There was plenty of traffic on the road: carts and wagons laden with farm produce trundled behind teams of mules or oxen, pedlars bowed under the load of their wares, a handful of riders, usually well dressed, and many travellers on foot.

'There're a lot of people on the road,' Marcus mused. 'Wonder why?'

147

A man walking past them carrying a big net filled with straw hats glanced back. 'No mystery in that, my friend. The governor is putting on a spectacle. Five days of entertainment in the arena. They're just putting the finishing touches to it, over there.' He pointed to a large wooden structure just outside the city.

Straining his eyes, Marcus could just make out the workmen swarming over the arena. He turned to the man. 'What's on the programme?'

'Oh, the usual. Animal fights, acrobats, execution of criminals and gladiators.' The pedlar patted his netting. 'And plenty of customers for me!'

Festus frowned. 'That means there won't be any rooms. Or at least not for a reasonable rate.'

'Perhaps we won't need to find a room,' said Marcus.

Lupus looked at him. 'What do you mean?'

'I think it's time we made use of Caesar's letter of introduction. We'll go to the governor and ask for information about Decimus and his estate. At the same time we can ask for accommodation in his palace. He's hardly likely to turn us down once he knows about the letter.'

'I'm not sure that's a good idea,' Festus replied. 'It means we won't be able to keep a low profile. You know what public

148

officials are like. Anybody who is anybody will know that we've arrived in Athens in a matter of days.'

Marcus shrugged. 'Maybe, but I'm tired. I'd find it hard to turn down a comfortable bed and a good meal right now.'

Festus shook his head. 'I'd rather as few people knew we were in Athens as possible. Word might reach Decimus.'

'If he comes looking for us, then that suits me,' Marcus said wearily. 'The sooner I face him and put an end to all this, the better.'

'Use your head, Marcus. It's a risk.'

'Risk?' Marcus laughed bitterly. 'Don't you think we've taken plenty of risks already? What's one more?'

Festus saw that his young companion was too tired to think clearly. They all needed a rest, somewhere they would be safe and comfortable. Perhaps Marcus was right about approaching the governor. But Festus could not help feeling anxious about it. He let out a sigh. 'All right. I just hope it won't be a mistake.'

Once they had passed inside the walls the smell of the crowded city instantly reminded Marcus of Rome. The narrow streets were just as winding and covered in sewage and rubbish. Most of the people had well-worn clothes and the same pinched, hungry expressions as the poorest people in Rome. They asked for directions to the governor's palace and were directed to an elaborate complex of buildings with ornate gardens, nestling beneath the Acropolis. The governor's quarters were arranged round an inner courtyard and the entrance was guarded by two soldiers, standing at ease as they held their spears and shields. As Marcus led his companions up to the entrance, the guards advanced their spears and one of them addressed him loudly.

'What's your business here?'

'We wish to see the governor,' Marcus said boldly. 'As soon as possible.'

The guard looked them over and shook his head. 'Not possible. Caius Servillus is not in the habit of making himself available to common pedlars, even if they are Roman. Now be on your way.'

Festus stepped forward to intervene but Marcus waved him back as he gave the guard a frosty look. 'What is your name, soldier?'

'My name?' The man chuckled. 'You don't need my name, sonny. What you need is to get lost. Now. Before my friend and I decide to box your ears.'

Marcus was not cowed by the man's threat. 'And you need a civil tongue in your head. I'll ask you once again. What is your name?'

This time the guard laughed. 'Who's asking?'

'Marcus Cornelius, and . . .' He reached inside his tunic and brought out a leather tube. Flipping the cap, he drew out Caesar's letter of introduction and unrolled it so that his seal was visible. 'Caius Julius Caesar. I assume you are familiar with the name?'

The soldier's laughter died away. He leaned forward to inspect the document. His eyes moved in the puzzled, haphazard manner of the illiterate but he was clearly impressed by the seal and the neat, official presentation. Even so, Marcus thought, he could just as easily have had Lupus knock something up and the guard would not have known any better.

'Er, right then,' the guard said uncertainly. 'I'd better take you in to see one of his officials.' He cocked a head at Lupus and Festus. 'They with you?'

'They are.'

The guard sighed. 'Then all of you had better follow me. Come on.'

He turned and muttered to the other guard that he would return as soon as he could, then beckoned to Marcus and his two friends. They passed through the gatehouse into a colonnaded courtyard lined with neatly trimmed potted shrubs. Ahead lay the imposing quarters of the Roman governor of the province of Achaea, three storeys high with marble columns supporting an imposing entrance hall. The guard approached a thin man in a tunic sitting on a small bench to one side of the hall and explained the presence of the three visitors before hurrying back to his post. The governor's servant looked at them doubtfully, until Marcus produced Caesar's letter, and then shrugged.

'Sirs, the governor can't see you today. He's at the arena, overseeing the final preparations for the spectacle.'

'Then we'll wait.'

'But he won't be back until very late. He's attending a feast of the philosophers' guild. Those events can go on for some time . . .'

Marcus clenched his jaw in frustration.

'You could come back tomorrow,' the servant suggested hopefully.

'No. We'll wait.'

The servant pursed his lips in irritation before he spoke again. 'I could find out if his aide will see you. If you wish.'

'Yes. That will do.'

'Please wait here.' The servant bowed his head and disappeared into a corridor leading off the hall.

Once he had gone Festus cleared his throat. 'What do you intend to say to this aide of the governor?'

'I'll tell him why we are here and ask for accommodation, of course.'

'Might be better to tell him no more than you need to. It is always best to keep those in the know to a small number in my experience.'

'But if the governor's aide is his right-hand man, then what's the danger?' asked Marcus.

Festus continued in a patient tone. 'Marcus, I've been dealing with these people since before you were born. If there's anything I've learned along the way it's that you have to be careful who you trust with what you know.'

Marcus knew that his friend was right, but at the same time he felt driven to take short cuts to find out where his mother was held. He should trust Festus's judgement, he told himself. Festus had never let him down. He was as wise as he was deadly and Marcus was fortunate to have him at hand. Even so, the urge to find his mother as swiftly as possible was eating away at his caution.

He heard footsteps and turned to see the servant returning with a slender man, who looked the same age as Festus. His dark hair was neatly cut and he had a finely trimmed beard along the line of his jaw, which met in a precise triangle beneath his mouth. As he approached, he smiled and held his hand out to Festus.

'Welcome to you, and your boys! I am the personal aide to Governor Servillus. My name is Quintus Euraeus. I am at your service. First, if I may, your letter of introduction?'

Festus nodded towards Marcus. 'Caesar entrusted the letter to this boy. He is the reason why we are in Athens. My name is Festus. Caesar sent me along to protect Marcus, and advise him.'

Euraeus's dark eyes flitted over Marcus and then Lupus. 'And the other boy?'

'I am Lupus, scribe to Caesar and friend of Marcus,' he announced proudly.

'Indeed. Then you are all most welcome. Now, if I might see the document?'

Marcus took out the letter again and handed it to Euraeus. The aide unrolled the letter, examined the seal and quickly ran his eyes over the contents. He handed it back to Marcus with a smile. 'It seems very comprehensive. Clearly Caesar holds you in high regard to gift you the authority to ask any favour in his name. I wonder why?'

'I served him well. Along with my friends here,' Marcus explained simply.

The aide waited in vain for him to elaborate, and then nodded. 'Evidently. Now, if you would be so kind as to follow me to my humble office, then let me know how I may help you.'

14

'So, Marcus, what can the governor, and I, do for you exactly?'
Euraeus smiled as he faced his three visitors across his gleaming
walnut desk. They were seated on the stools that one of the
aide's clerks had brought for them, along with a tray of scented
water and some pastries.

Marcus hastily chewed the mouthful of minted lamb and
crust that he had been enjoying and wiped the crumbs from his
mouth. At the same time his mind was hurriedly organizing
his thoughts over how much information he should provide to
Euraeus. Marcus explained the cover story that they had agreed
on and then moved on to the real reason for their presence in
Greece.

'Caesar sent us here to find someone. A slave.' He felt a
twinge of pain as he used the word to describe his mother. 'She

is the – property – of a moneylender and tax collector who has an estate here in Greece.'

'I see.' Euraeus nodded. 'And what does Caesar want you to do when you find this slave?'

Festus coughed a warning. 'Marcus –'

'Set her free.' Marcus's voice caught and he forced himself to control his emotions as he continued. 'She is being held illegally. Kidnapped by the man who now claims to own her.'

Euraeus stroked his jaw. 'This is a serious crime you speak of. A serious accusation at any rate. What proof is there that she was kidnapped? Were there any witnesses?'

'Yes.' Marcus felt a lump in his throat. 'There was one.'

'That helps if we are to bring the perpetrator to justice. Speaking of which, do you know his name?'

Marcus nodded. 'Decimus.'

'Decimus?' The aide raised an eyebrow. 'I know a few moneylenders by that name, none of whom strike me as particularly criminal.'

'Really?' Festus interrupted with a wry grin. 'Seems you have a higher standard of moneylender here in Greece than I ever met back in Rome.'

'There are many things in Greece that are of a higher standard than in Rome,' Euraeus replied with a smile. 'Our civilization being one of them. But back to the business at hand. Obviously we need to find the right Decimus to bring to justice. Do you have any other information about him that would help me?'

'Only that he has an estate in the Peloponnese.'

'Hmmm. That's not much to go on.'

'It's a start,' Lupus added. 'There must surely be a record of the taxes due on estates in the province. Then it's only a question of matching the records to the names and we should find the man easily.'

'Oh, there are records all right. The trouble is they are at the fiscal procurator's office down at Piraeus. I'll have to send for them. They could be brought here in a matter of days, once the procurator returns to Athens.'

'Where is he?' asked Marcus, stifling his impatience.

'He was called away to resolve a tax dispute in Thebes. Shouldn't take long.'

'Well, couldn't we look at his records before he gets back?'

Euraeus looked shocked. 'Such records are confidential, my dear boy. It would be unthinkable to make them available to anyone behind the procurator's back. It's more than my job is worth to even suggest it. No, I'm afraid you must wait until he returns.'

'What about the governor?' Festus interjected. 'Surely he has the necessary authority?'

The aide thought a moment and nodded slowly. 'True. He might agree to it. But Servillus won't be available until the morning. At least. Later if he's been in his cups. I suggest you come back tomorrow at noon.'

'That raises another matter,' said Festus. 'We need somewhere to stay while we are in Athens. That won't be easy with the crowds who have come to see the governor's spectacle. You can arrange something for us here, I trust? Some accommodation and some food.'

Euraeus shook his head and made a sad expression. 'Unfortunately, there is no spare room at the palace for the same reason.'

Festus leaned to the side and tapped a finger on the leather tube hanging from a thong round Marcus's neck. 'I think that will disappoint the man we work for.'

The aide considered this briefly and coughed. 'On second thoughts, I'm sure I can arrange something for the three of you.'

'That's better.' Festus smiled.

'Now *that* is a nice mattress,' Lupus grinned as he tested the bed on either side of him. 'I think this might be the best night's sleep since we arrived in Greece.'

Marcus nodded absently as he stood looking through the window across the palace gardens and over the city. Night had fallen and the full moon cast a pale blue glow over the tiled roofs that stretched round the palace complex. Euraeus had provided them with a comfortable room in a wing used to accommodate those travelling on official business. A small kitchen in the mess hall on the ground floor provided drink and food for guests of the governor, and they had eaten their fill and retired for the night. Marcus felt a warm glow of contentment – not just because of the creature comforts they were enjoying after many days on the road, but tomorrow they would seek help from Governor Servillus to find the estate of Decimus. If Lupus was right, it would be a straightforward process, then Marcus might finally be reunited with his mother. The only danger being that Decimus might be forewarned of their presence in Greece.

As he gazed up at the moon a memory of her scent flooded him with the fuller memory of home and the happiness he had once known. He held on to the feeling while behind him the others climbed into their beds and settled. Soon the light snores of Festus and the softer breathing of Lupus drifted from the darkness, and Marcus could enjoy his thoughts in blissful solitude, letting his eyes close as he recalled his mother's face in detail, and that of Titus, standing behind her, his craggy features split by a warm smile. Marcus felt his heart lurch and was surprised by the depth of his feeling for the old soldier who had raised him. Titus may not have been his real father, but Marcus loved him all the same.

Then he imagined another figure, the shadowy figure of Spartacus. He had no face, just a looming presence that was somehow dangerous and threatening. Marcus could feel no stirring of his heart for the man whose blood he shared, and the only bond seemed to be ideas of duty and destiny. Perhaps if things had been different he might have loved Spartacus as much as he had loved Titus. In return Spartacus may have been as fond and proud of him as Titus had been. But then he knew such a life would have been impossible. Spartacus had been a slave. Even if there had been no revolt there would have been no prospect of a happy life. Gladiators lived to fight and die. Any children they had were little more than another entry on the list of their owner's property. Marcus would never have known freedom as he grew up, just the endless routine grind of hard toil. As it was, he knew the value of freedom, and knew what the loss of it meant.

The next morning Marcus and the others rose long after sunrise and ate a leisurely breakfast before returning to the governor's offices. They had put on their best tunics and cleaned their boots in order to give a good impression to Servillus. A decent night's sleep and a full belly did much to improve their spirits as they walked through the gardens towards the administration building. Once they had passed inside a clerk took them to the office of Euraeus. The Greek greeted them with a ready smile.

'Good day, gentlemen. I trust you found your accommodation adequate?'

Festus nodded. 'Very comfortable, thank you.'

'Is the governor ready to see us?' Marcus asked impatiently.

A look of sorrow flickered across Euraeus's face as he clasped his hands together. 'Alas, no. His excellency has not yet risen. His servant says that he is not likely to stir for another hour or two at least. But rest assured, as soon as he reaches his office I will tell him your request is urgent.'

Marcus sighed with disappointment, shifting his weight from one foot to the other until Festus squeezed his shoulder gently.

'You've waited two years for this, Marcus. What does an hour or so matter?'

Every instant that separated Marcus from his mother pained him, but he forced himself to nod. 'I suppose.'

'Good!' Euraeus beamed. 'I suggest that you return to your

162

quarters and wait there. I'll send for you the moment the governor is available.'

Marcus nodded and he and his friends turned to leave the office. They returned through the gardens to the guest accommodation wing and were about to enter when Lupus stopped and cleared his throat.

'Er, would you mind if I took a quick look around the city?'

Marcus turned to him. 'You heard Euraeus. He told us to wait here.'

'I know, but he said it could be some time before we are sent for. I'll be back before then. I promise.'

Festus looked uncertain and Lupus decided to press his case. 'I've dreamt of visiting Athens. It'd be a shame not to see anything of it before we leave the city. I won't be long.'

Marcus could not help smiling at his desperate expression. 'Go on then. See what you have to, but don't hang about.'

Before Festus could protest Lupus had nodded his thanks and was striding towards the entrance of the palace complex. The bodyguard let out a frustrated breath.

'I hope nothing happens to him.'

'He'll be safe enough,' Marcus smiled. 'If he can cope with the streets of Rome, then he can cope here. Besides, he's picked up a few useful skills on the road. Lupus will be fine.'

'I hope so,' Festus muttered as he followed Marcus up the stairs into the accommodation wing.

There was not a cloud in the sky and the sun blazed down on Athens from deep, peaceful blue heavens. Lupus made his way through the busy main streets towards the stepped path of the Panathanaic Way, climbing up from the city to the great rock of the Acropolis that dominated Athens. He passed through the gate into the temple complex, excitedly looking at statues and buildings he had read about when he was growing up in Rome. He knew there was little time and made directly for the Parthenon where he wandered around the vast structure, marvelling at the elaborate painted frieze that ran along the top of the columns. As his neck began to ache, Lupus made his way to the parapet and leaned on it, gazing across the city and the flat plane beyond towards the distant sea that sparkled in the sunlight. He sighed with contentment as he enjoyed the view.

He knew that his time in the city would be brief, but he did not resent it since it would mean that Marcus's quest would soon come to an end. While the prospect of finding Marcus's mother was a happy one, Lupus knew that it would mean an end to the fellowship of the three of them. Marcus would remain with his mother while Festus and Lupus returned to

Caesar's house in Rome. In truth Lupus had enjoyed being on the road, away from the stinking confines of a city. He had even begun to enjoy his daily sessions of exercise and weapons training.

The sun had reached its zenith and Lupus knew he must rejoin his friends. With a sigh he tore himself away from the spectacular view and made his way back across the Acropolis to the gate and the path that descended into the city. At the bottom he turned on to the crowded street that led to the governor's palace. At once the familiar smells of crowded humanity assaulted his nose, and the shouts of traders and the city's inhabitants filled his ears. Lupus threaded his way through the crowd and was in sight of the entrance to the palace when he heard a cry from ahead of him.

'Make way there! Make way!'

The calls grew louder and now Lupus could see a tall, well-built man with a staff clearing a path for the litter that came behind him. Eight slaves carried the poles that supported the covered litter. The occupant was concealed behind the thin linen curtains that hung from the frame. Lupus joined the others who squeezed to the side of the street to get out of the way of the man with the staff, who used it to sweep pedestrians aside.

165

'Make way!' he shouted again. 'Make way for Gaius Amelius Decimus!'

Lupus froze. At once he was jostled from behind.

'Oi! Watch yourself, boy!' A man pressed past him with an angry expression. 'Don't get in people's way. You damned nuisance.'

Lupus mumbled an apology and retreated into the doorway of a bread shop. He stared at the litter as it passed by. A slight jostle disturbed the curtain and he caught a glimpse of a hand, with heavy gold rings on it.

'Make way for Decimus!' the slave with the staff intoned again.

'Scum . . .' a voice growled and Lupus turned to see the baker at his shoulder. He ignored Lupus and stared hatefully at the litter. 'Money-grabbing Roman leech.'

There was no doubt in Lupus's mind. This was the Decimus they were searching for. Right here in Athens. No more than a hundred paces from the entrance to the governor's palace! His mind raced. He thought of running to the palace to tell his friends. Then he realized it was more important to follow Decimus and discover where the tax collector lived.

The litter continued down the street as Lupus began to follow it. They passed through the heart of the city before climbing a street to a more elevated area in a wealthier neighbourhood. The close-packed houses gave way to larger homes with imposing entrances before the street opened out on to a market where traders sold spices and other luxury goods. The litter stopped at a short flight of steps leading to a studded door where a watchman sat. At first sight of the litter, he rushed down and bowed his head, then stood ready to hand his master down from the litter. Lupus paused by one of the stalls so he could watch without attracting attention. The light curtains of the litter were swept aside as the occupant swung his legs out, and the wigless head of Decimus gleamed in the sunlight. He glanced round quickly before he climbed the stairs. The door opened for him and he disappeared into the house. A moment later the slaves carrying the litter continued on, turning into a narrow side alley as they made for the slave quarters at the rear.

His heart pounding with excitement, Lupus turned and raced back to the palace, raising cries of protest as he barged his way through the crowds. At the entrance to the palace he breathlessly explained his business to the guard who waved him inside. Lupus could barely wait to relate his discovery to his friends. Entering the guest accommodation, he took the stairs three at a time to the second floor and raced down the cool corridor towards their room. The door was ajar and he thrust it aside as he burst in and stood, chest heaving from his exertion.

Then he frowned. He had fully expected to see Festus and Marcus. Instead there were two soldiers waiting. They wore the red tunics of the legions, together with heavy boots and short swords hanging from thick leather straps across their shoulders.

'Where are my friends?' Lupus demanded. 'There's something I have to tell them!'

'You can tell them, all right.' One of the soldiers grinned as he stepped forward and grasped Lupus's arm.

'Hey!' he protested, and tried to pull himself free. 'What do you think you're doing? Let go of me!'

But the soldier just tightened his grip and bunched his spare hand into a fist that he raised threateningly. 'Stop struggling, or I'll give you a thick ear, boy!'

Lupus reluctantly did as he was told and the second soldier took his other arm, then he was led into the corridor.

'Just tell me what's going on. Where are Marcus and Festus?'

'You'll find out soon enough.'

'Where are you taking me? What's going on?'

'You know well enough, lad.' The soldier glanced at him with a cold expression. 'Don't play the innocent with me.'

168

Lupus was confused and afraid. 'I have no idea what this is about.'

The soldier sniffed dismissively. 'Of course not. That's what all criminals say.'

'Criminals?' Lupus felt his heart lurch. 'What are you talking about?'

'You and your friends are under arrest. For murder.'

15

The cell was small, dark and airless, and the only light came from a narrow slit high up on one wall. Together with a handful of other cells it had been constructed under some storerooms at the rear of the palace, away from the garden and out of earshot so that those being held would not disturb those who lived and worked in the palace. Unlike the previous night there were no comforts for the prisoners. Instead of beds there was just a pile of straw in one corner, a slop bucket and a small grille beneath the door where food and water were passed to the prisoners. Outside there was a narrow passage with three cells on each side. A single jailer had a small room beside the stairs leading up from the prison.

Marcus and Festus had been thrown into the cell over an hour before Lupus joined them, and their relief at being reunited was short-lived as they considered their situation.

'Murder, he said.' Lupus shook his head. 'What murder? Do you think it has something to do with that slave auctioneer, Pindarus?'

'What else could it be?' Festus replied as he tested the door, grasping the bars in the grille and giving it a good shake. The hinges rattled and squealed but the door was solid enough.

'Hey!' the jailer called from the end of the passage. 'Leave that alone. I'm responsible for the fittings, I am. You do any damage to 'em and there'll be no rations for you lot!'

Festus stepped back and slumped on the straw next to the others. 'We're in trouble. Deep trouble.'

'But how can we be?' asked Marcus. 'How can they have connected us to what happened in Stratos? It has to be something else . . . Someone's made a mistake. As soon as it's discovered we'll be out of here.'

Festus shrugged. 'I hope you're right that this is a mistake, Marcus. But this smacks of something else.'

Lupus started. He had been so preoccupied with the sudden reverse that he had forgotten the news he had for his friends.

'Decimus. It must be something to do with him. I saw him a short time ago.'

Marcus turned to him, his eyes intent. 'What d'you mean?'

171

Lupus briefly described what he had seen as the others listened closely.

'I was rushing back to tell you when I was arrested,' Lupus concluded.

Marcus rubbed his jaw thoughtfully. 'Which way was the litter heading?'

'Down the street. In the opposite direction to the governor's palace.'

'Then it's likely he was here and I fear he is behind this, like you say. The question is, how did he know we had arrived in Athens?'

'How do you think?' Festus responded flatly. 'I told you that few secrets are kept in a place like this. We turned up, with you waving Caesar's letter of introduction and explaining our business, so word was bound to get out. The only surprise is that it happened so quickly. Decimus must have spies everywhere.'

Marcus bowed his head for a moment. He had made a mistake in coming to the governor's palace. He had let his impatience and frustration get the better of him and now all three of them had paid the price for his folly. Marcus cleared his throat and spoke quietly. 'I'm so sorry. I should have been more cautious. It's my fault.'

'That's true,' Festus responded coldly. 'But it doesn't change anything. We're in here and we need to get out. The question is, how? Escape is out of the question. The door's solid and we have no friends in Athens to help spring us from this cell. We're stuck. The only chance we have is to try and talk our way out of it when the governor hears our case.'

'How can you be sure he will?'

'Because I'm a Roman citizen, and you have Caesar's letter of introduction. All three of us are connected to Caesar. Only the governor of a province can sentence a Roman citizen for a crime.'

'What about me?' asked Lupus. 'I'm only a freedman. Not a citizen.'

'You're with Marcus and me. That should cover you. Besides, that's not the point. We only have to be put in front of the governor. Then we can explain ourselves and hopefully get out of this mess.'

Marcus nodded. 'And get our hands on Decimus.'

The bodyguard clicked his tongue. 'That's not going to be so easy. He knows we're after him now. Even if we get off the murder charge he'll be sure to surround himself with men to protect him. More likely he'll leave Athens and run for cover.'

Marcus considered this briefly. 'His estate.'

'That's my guess. And we won't have the element of surprise any more. It's going to be tough.'

There was a brief silence before Lupus spoke. 'Aren't we getting a bit ahead of ourselves?' He slapped his hand against the cold stone wall. 'We have to get out of here first.'

Festus pursed his lips. 'You're right. No point in looking too far ahead. We'll have to bide our time until the governor hears our case.'

'How long will that take?' asked Marcus.

'Hard to say. This spectacle he's throwing for the local people will occupy most of his time until it's over. We might have to wait here until then, and then a bit longer as he catches up with the backlog. On the other hand, if Servillus is an efficient man, he might want to get it out of the way before the spectacle begins.'

Lupus stared round the grim cell with a look of horror. 'You mean we might be in here for several days?'

'It's likely. Better make yourself comfortable.'

Lupus pulled his knees up under his chin and stared in misery at the opposite wall. Marcus was still feeling guilty about having put his own needs above the safety of his comrades. Even though Festus had a fatalistic attitude to their plight, Marcus could not let himself shake off the blame so easily and sat brooding. The hours passed and the shaft of light that came through the slit slowly traced its way along the wall until the sun dipped behind the palace, leaving them in gloomy shadows.

It was two hours after sunset, as near as Marcus could estimate, that they heard footsteps in the passage outside as several men approached the cell. The flicker of light from a torch lit up the bars of the grille. An iron bolt on the outside grated back and the hinges groaned as the jailer thrust the door open.

'On yer feet, you lot! They've come fer you.'

He stepped aside as an optio ducked his head into the cell, torch in hand, and his nose wrinkling at the stench before he gestured to the prisoners.

'Outside.'

Marcus and the others exchanged anxious glances as they rose quickly and followed the optio into the passage. A section of soldiers lined one side and four turned to lead the way while the other four followed the optio and the prisoners, escorting them towards the steps at the other end of the passage.

'Shall I keep the cell fer 'em then?' the jailer called out.

The optio glanced back and replied sourly, 'You'll be told in good time. Meanwhile get the straw changed and slop it out.'

'What? There'll be an extra charge fer that! I ain't runnin' a bloody charity house here, yer know!'

The optio ignored his rant and the party climbed the stairs to emerge in the moonlit yard behind the palace.

'Where are you taking us?' asked Marcus.

'Shut your mouth,' the optio snapped. 'You'll speak when spoken to and not before. Clear? That goes for all of you.'

They proceeded in silence across the yard and through a small door at the rear of the palace. After following a corridor lit by oil lamps, they climbed a flight of stairs into a wider thoroughfare where a few clerks and palace slaves bustled to and fro. At the end of that corridor was an impressive doorway guarded by two more soldiers. As they approached, the optio nodded his head and the guards grasped the handles to swing the doors open. Marcus glanced through the gap between the soldiers striding ahead and saw a large chamber beyond, lit by candles set at intervals along the wall. At the far end was a dais with a large desk on it. To one side a clerk was setting out his writing materials, while a slave placed a glass jar of wine and a silver cup on the desk.

The optio marched his party across the hall, their boots echoing off the high walls, and halted in front of the dais. He waved Marcus and the others forward.

'Stand there. In line, facing the dais.'

They did as they were told and the soldiers formed up behind them. Then there was quiet, except for the clerk busily rubbing down a wax slate in readiness for the notes he would be taking shortly. The slave who had brought the wine and cup left the chamber, disappearing through a small door at the side. Once the clerk had finished his preparations all was still and silent. Marcus stood and waited, wondering what they were doing in the chamber. He risked a glance at Festus and cocked an eyebrow, but Festus simply shrugged.

'Eyes front, you!' the optio barked and Marcus quickly did as he was told.

They were not kept waiting long. Footsteps approached down the corridor behind them, then entered the chamber. A large man in an elaborately embroidered tunic climbed the steps on to the dais and moved round to take the chair behind the desk. Behind him came Euraeus, clutching a scroll and a few waxed tablets under his arm. Once he was settled the fat man cleared his throat and addressed the small gathering.

'I am Governor Servillus, present to hear the case of those accused of the murder of Pindarus of Stratos.'

So, Festus was right, Marcus admitted to himself as the clerk scratched down the opening remarks.

The governor gestured towards Euraeus. 'The particulars of the case, if you please.'

'Yes, your excellency.' Euraeus bowed his head, then opened one of the waxed tablets as he consulted his notes. 'Two days ago a report reached the palace of the murder of a slave auctioneer in Stratos some days earlier. He was found dead in his garden and had been struck on the head. His servants reported that they had disturbed robbers who had broken into the house of Pindarus. The magistrates of the city described the suspects as being a man and two youths, strangers to the town. They disappeared after the killing had taken place. A few days after that there was another incident reported relating to an event at Leuctra where a man and two boys were involved in a fight in the town market. And then yesterday these three individuals turned up in Athens. They entered the palace and requested an audience with your excellency. I explained that you were busy with your duties and they would have to wait until later. It was then that I recalled the news from Stratos and decided to offer them accommodation in the guest quarters where an eye could be kept on them while I investigated the matter further. After I heard of the event in Leuctra I gave the order for their arrest and for them to be charged with the murder of Pindarus.'

Euraeus concluded his overview and looked up from his notes. The governor stared at Marcus and the others as he considered the information and then he wagged a fleshy finger at his official.

'You have done well, Euraeus. Quick thinking.'

'Thank you, your excellency. But I was only doing my humble duty.'

'Of course you were. You're a damned conscientious fellow. Wish there were more like you on my staff.'

'Your excellency is too kind.'

The governor turned his attention back to the accused. 'Well? What have you to say for yourselves, eh? Speak up!'

Festus took a deep breath. 'We are innocent, sir. We did not murder Pindarus.'

'Of course not,' Servillus said. 'But that's what all murderers say.'

'Sir, if we had murdered the man, and were on the run, then what good reason could we have for turning up on your doorstep and asking to see you?'

The governor sniffed. 'Why don't you tell me?'

'Very well. As we informed your official over there, we have come to Greece in search of a woman, the wife of a retired legionary officer, who had been kidnapped and is believed to be on the estate of a tax collector and moneylender by the name of Decimus.'

'Decimus?' The governor's eyebrows rose in surprise. 'My good friend, Decimus? How can that be? The man is an honest chap. Pillar of the community and all that. Why, he was only here earlier today to make a most generous contribution towards the costs of the spectacle I am providing for the people of this city. You dare to accuse him of kidnapping?'

Festus continued in a calm tone. 'If the woman concerned is indeed held among the other slaves owned by Decimus, then he is committing a serious crime, sir. That is why Caesar, my master, sent us here to search for her and see to it that she is set free, and that those responsible for her kidnapping are brought to account.'

'Caesar sent you?' Servillus laughed mockingly. 'Look at you. You appear and stink like common vagrants.'

'That is because we have been held in one of your cells for much of the day, sir.'

The governor ignored the comment as he leaned forward and pointed at Festus. 'You are a liar. The very idea that you represent Julius Caesar is laughable.'

'But we can prove it!' Marcus blurted out. 'I have a document signed by Caesar. A letter of introduction.'

'What's this?' Servillus demanded. 'Damned impudence!'

180

'Sir,' Euraeus intervened. 'This matter is easily resolved. If the boy claims to have such a letter, then let him produce it.'

'Indeed! So, boy, where is this document of yours, eh? Show it to me.'

'I can't, sir,' Marcus conceded. 'It's in a leather case in my pack, back in the guest room. If you let me fetch it this can all be settled and you'll see that we are telling the truth.'

'You'll do no such thing,' the governor snapped. 'Optio, you go. Search these scoundrels' baggage for this document and if you find it, bring it back here at once.'

'Yes, sir!' The optio saluted and strode out of the chamber, back down the corridor. The governor turned his attention to Marcus and the others. 'We'll know the truth soon enough. I warn you, if you are lying to me it will go ill with you.'

'I'm telling the truth,' Marcus said firmly. 'As you shall see.'

The governor poured himself a cup of wine and eased himself back in his chair, sipping occasionally, as they waited for the optio to return. Euraeus stood to one side with the faintest of smiles on his lips. Looking at him, Marcus had a vague sense of foreboding, but it instantly faded as he heard footsteps in the corridor. When the optio entered the chamber he strode across the tiled floor to the dais, halting in front of the desk to salute.

The governor lowered his cup and leaned forward. 'Well?'

'No sign of any letter, sir. Nor a leather case.'

Marcus felt his hopes sink like a stone. 'It was there. You must have found it!'

The optio glanced over his shoulder and scowled. 'There was nothing there. You lied.'

Marcus's jaw sagged and he turned to Festus. 'It was there. I know it. Tell him.'

Festus shook his head. 'It's too late, Marcus. We've been trapped. All very neat. I imagine this is all your doing, Euraeus.'

The Greek feigned surprise and touched a hand to his chest. 'Me? You accuse me?'

'How much did Decimus reward you for your services, I wonder?'

Servillus slapped his hand down on the table. 'Enough of your nonsense! This little drama of yours is over. There is no letter. You are not here on Caesar's business and you clearly think me a fool who can be sold such a pack of lies. Well, I tell you, I am no fool and I can see the truth clearly enough. The three of you are the men who robbed Pindarus, and killed him when he caught you in the act. You fled Stratos and came here thinking to trick me into providing you with food and a roof over your heads while you hid from justice. Now justice has found you out, and you will pay the price for your crimes.' He paused and looked at each of them in turn before he smiled cruelly.

Marcus could not help trembling as he awaited his fate.

'There is only one fit punishment for your crimes. That, three days from now, on the second day of the spectacle you three shall be taken from your cell to the arena and there tied to stakes before wild animals are released to tear you apart, for the sake of justice, and the pleasure of the mob.'

16

'Condemned to the beasts . . . .' Lupus moaned quietly to himself as he sat squeezed into the corner of the cell. 'Sweet Gods, spare us . . . Spare us.'

The sun had risen shortly before and a thin shaft of light had penetrated the gloom, illuminating the grim scene once again for those in the cold, stinking confines of the small space. It had been a miserable night for the three prisoners once they had been roughly shoved back through the narrow entrance and the door to the cell thudded behind them. The iron bolt had rasped home and the footsteps of the soldiers and the jailer had receded, then there was a brief silence before Festus slumped on to the straw with a dry rustle. Marcus stood by the door for a moment in the darkness, scarcely able to believe the fate that lay in store for them. He heard Lupus trying to stifle his sobs in the far corner and felt some pity for his friend.

Marcus had already faced death in the arena. He had also learned that it did no good to allow himself to be paralysed by fear. Fear changed nothing. All a person could do was choose whether to surrender to that fear, or deal with it and continue the struggle. That was fine as far as it was possible to fight, Marcus reminded himself, but they would be tied to stakes while being torn apart by wild animals. They would be quite helpless and could only pray that it was all over quickly.

He turned away from the door and felt his way along the wall to the pile of straw at the rear of the cell, trying not to imagine the slavering jaws of the beasts as they tore into his flesh. As he felt the straw give under his feet Marcus lowered himself into it and curled into a ball to try and sleep. There was no sound apart from the easy breathing of Festus and the faint choked gasps of Lupus. No one felt like speaking, each in his own private world of despair. For Marcus, whose failure would also condemn his mother to the hell of permanent slavery, the sense of guilt was almost as hard to bear as his fear of the horrific death awaiting him.

★

By the morning, some of the fear and misery had faded from his mind and he looked up as a wooden tray scraped through the gap at the bottom of the door.

'Here's your rations,' the jailer growled from outside. 'Eat 'em up. Don't want to disappoint the beasts with some half-starved streaks of nothing!'

He laughed harshly to himself as he shuffled away along the passage.

Festus crossed the room to pick up the tray and bring it back to the two boys sitting on the straw. There was a loaf of dried bread, some hard cheese and a cooked bone with some meat still attached to it, besides a jug of water. He broke the bread and cheese into roughly equal portions and pressed them into the hands of the boys. Marcus took his readily and made himself chew on the crust of his bread. Lupus simply stared down at the food in his lap until Festus leaned over and put his hand on the youth's shoulder.

'You have to eat.'

'Why? What's the point?'

'You have to keep your strength up. We might find a way out of this.'

Lupus laughed nervously. 'How? How can we get out? We're finished, Festus. It's over. We're going to die.'

Festus clenched his fingers into the boy's shoulders and

186

gritted his teeth as he spoke with cold determination. 'We ain't dead until we're dead. Anything can happen between now and the day they plan to take us into the arena. If anything does happen then you need to be in a fit state to respond to events. Understand? Now eat your food.'

Lupus pursed his lips, then reluctantly tore a corner from his portion of bread and began to chew.

'That's better.' Festus nodded. 'Don't give up hope.'

They ate in silence and since neither of the boys was keen on the bone Festus shrugged and took it for himself, working his teeth hard to tear off what meat there was on the joint. Afterwards he made Lupus and Marcus get up and carry out a set of exercises, pushing the scribe hard in order to keep his mind occupied and tire his body out. As the sun reached its zenith Festus ended the session and the boys, sweating and breathing hard, collapsed on to the straw. Lupus had not slept the previous night and now, finally, exhaustion took hold of him and he was soon fast asleep.

'He's not coping with this,' Festus said quietly.

Marcus stretched his shoulders. 'Are you surprised? You think I'm coping?'

Festus turned to look at him searchingly. 'You're doing well enough, Marcus. You seem calm, under the circumstances.'

'You think?' Marcus lowered his head into his hands and his voice caught as he spoke in a low tone. 'I've failed. My mother will spend the rest of her days suffering. Starved, beaten and never knowing what happened to me.' He swallowed hard, feeling the urge to surrender to his grief, to slip back into his childhood and be looked after. He craved a return to that life. But it was gone. Even if, by some miracle, he escaped from the death sentence, his experiences had changed him. Marcus had discovered too much about the darkness of this world to ever be free of that knowledge. It was as if a part of him had already died and he grieved for that small boy he had once been. 'I've failed . . .'

Festus shook his head. 'Marcus, it's not as simple as that. If you had failed then you would have been defeated long before now. You would never have survived the gladiator school and that Celt, Ferax. Nor any of the other perils that you have faced, and triumphed over. No, you have held true to your course and your mother would be proud of you. Your father too, if he were alive.' Festus smiled fondly. 'If I'd had a son like you I would have been just as proud.'

'What good is that to me now? It's over, Festus.'

'Not until you draw your last breath. That's how it is for gladiators, of all people. And you, Marcus, are a gladiator through and through. Perhaps the finest I have ever known. If – when – you grow into a man, then you will become a legend. I am certain of it.'

Marcus turned to look at him, a faint spark of hope and determination rekindling in his heart. He forced himself to smile at his companion, and friend. 'Thank you.'

'Be strong, Marcus. Not just for yourself, but for Lupus too, and me.'

Marcus drew a deep, calming breath and nodded. 'I will.'

The jailer returned for the tray and water jug late at dusk. He was not alone. Two soldiers came with him and stood, hands resting on the handles of their swords, as the door opened and the jailer pointed to Marcus.

'You, pick up the tray and bring it here.'

Marcus did as he was told then crossed the cell and held the tray out. The jailer took it then stepped back into the passage. 'Outside.'

Marcus hesitated and narrowed his eyes suspiciously. 'Why?'

'Do as you're told and don't cheek me. Not unless you want a hiding.'

'Wait!' Festus called out, rising to his feet. 'What do you want with him?'

'None of your business!' the jailer snapped as he reached for Marcus's shoulder and grabbed him firmly before wrenching him through the door. At once he slammed the door shut and slid the bolt back just before Festus reached the grille and clasped his fingers round the iron bars.

'What's going on?'

The jailer snatched the small club from his belt and held it up. 'Back off! Or I'll break your fingers.'

Festus released his grip and retreated. The two soldiers took Marcus firmly by the arms and led him down the passage towards the steps.

'Where are you taking me?' he demanded.

'You'll see,' one of the soldiers replied. 'Someone wants a word with you.'

They climbed the steps into the yard behind the palace and steered Marcus towards a stable where a figure stood in the shadowed interior. In the light from a small torch burning in a bracket Marcus recognized the man waiting for them.

'Decimus.'

It was months since he had last seen the man, in the secret valley of the Apennines where they'd been held by the slave rebels led by Brixus. Decimus had been dishevelled and afraid then. Now his features were comfortably filled out, and he wore a neatly styled wig with oiled ringlets. The very picture of a rich and powerful man, his tunic was cut from expensive cloth and his boots were fine, soft calf's leather. He smiled with satisfaction as Marcus stood before him, grasped on each side by the two soldiers.

'I wondered if we would meet again, son of Titus.'

Now it seemed there was nothing to lose, Marcus was tempted to tell Decimus the truth about his father. But he realized that could worsen the situation for his mother, if she still lived. And there would be wider repercussions if it became known that Spartacus had fathered a son. It would send a shiver through the hearts of Roman slave owners, who would treat their slaves even more harshly.

'It was always my intention to find you,' Marcus answered coolly. 'And to kill you once I had freed my mother.'

'Well now, that's not going to happen,' Decimus chuckled. 'In two days you will be dead. You and your friends. Torn to pieces. I'll be there to enjoy the moment when my revenge against your father is complete. It's been a long road since that day when he gave me this.' Decimus patted his leg, wounded by Titus, which had led to Decimus being discharged from the legion where they had both served. 'In a way, I should be grateful to your father. If I had stayed in the army I might have been

191

dead by now. As it was, it opened up a new life for me. I made my fortune and found a way into the ranks of the most powerful men in Rome. Be that as it may, I still wanted revenge. And now I have it. Titus is dead, you are about to join him, and your mother will be left to eke out what is left of her life.'

'Then she's alive,' said Marcus, a flush of relief surging through his heart.

'Of course. I wouldn't put an end to her suffering too soon. Right now, she languishes in chains on my estate in Laconia. I saw her when I was there a month ago.' He pretended to look concerned. 'She's not doing well, alas. Thin, dirty, a mere shadow of the person you once knew. You would be hard pressed to recognize her. A pity, she was a fine-looking woman once, and I dare say, a loving mother, eh?'

Marcus tried to take a step towards Decimus as a savage growl rumbled in his throat, but the soldiers tightened their grip. Decimus regarded him with an amused expression and then continued. 'I have to say, I am impressed by your persistence, young man. You've been something of a thorn in my side for a while now. Interfering with my schemes in Rome then coming here to hunt me down. I had no idea you were so close. Luckily, more than a few men on the governor's staff are in my pay. It was simple enough to arrange your arrest once I connected you to the murder in Stratos. That was your work, I assume?'

Marcus shook his head. 'We did not kill Pindarus. We are not murderers, like you.'

'Murderer?' Decimus made a hurt expression. 'I am a simple businessman, Marcus. I make money, lots of money. If that means removing someone who stands in my way, then that's too bad. It's not personal, you understand. Just sound business practice. But it's different for you and your family. Revenge is a very personal thing indeed. And I cannot tell you how much pleasure it gives me to see you suffer.'

'You won't get away with this. Caesar knows we are here. If he finds out what you have done then you're finished.'

'But he won't find out. As far as he will know you travelled to Greece and disappeared. And what the beasts leave will be thrown into a mass grave. Your belongings will be disposed of, starting with this.'

Decimus reached into his tunic and pulled out a scrolled document. He unrolled it so Marcus could see the signature and seal of Caesar. 'My friend, Euraeus, took the precaution of removing this from your room after you were arrested. Now it's time to destroy the evidence that gives your story any credibility.'

Decimus rolled the document up and moved towards the

torch. As he held the scroll to the flames Marcus could not help gasping. 'No . . .'

The end of the letter caught fire and Decimus held it in front of Marcus as the yellow tongues of flame lapped up the side of the letter, scorching it. The papyrus crackled briefly and turned black then started to crumble. Decimus released it just as the flames came near the tips of his fingers and it dropped to the floor where it burned out.

Marcus lifted his eyes from the small pile of blackened ashes and met Decimus's mocking smile. Something snapped inside him and released a torrent of pure rage. He let out a savage snarl and at the same time lifted his right boot and slammed it down on the toes at the end of the sandal of the man next to him. The soldier let out a gasp of pain and momentarily slackened his grip. Marcus wrenched his arm free and swung his fist round and struck the other man in the groin as hard as he could. The soldier doubled over with a groan and Marcus leapt at Decimus, fingers curved like claws. The man had no time to react, except to open his mouth to let out a cry, but it never came as Marcus piled into him, clamping his hands round Decimus's throat and squeezing with all his might. Decimus staggered back and caught his heel on the edge of a flagstone and fell on to his back. Marcus went with him, teeth bared, as he tried to throttle the life out of the man who had tormented him the last two years of his life.

Decimus recovered quickly from his shock and grabbed the boy's wrists, straining to pull them away from his throat as he gasped. 'For the Gods' sake, get this fiend off me!'

The first soldier limped over and bunched his hand into a fist. He raised it high, but Marcus was oblivious to the danger. His mad, glaring eyes were fixed rigidly on the face of the man beneath him. Then he felt a mighty blow to his temple and everything went white. But he still clung to his enemy. He never felt the second blow, only another blinding flash of light and then darkness and oblivion.

17

Marcus was still feeling groggy when the palace guards came to take the prisoners to the holding cage beneath the arena early the next morning. Festus and Lupus supported their friend between them and half carried, half dragged him out of the cell, up the stairs and out of the palace. The streets were packed with people making for the arena, eager to witness the first day of the spectacle. Families clutched little baskets of food and waterskins to see them through the day's entertainment. Groups of loud young men compared the merits of the gladiators who would take part in the contests in the last stage of the event. The guards and their prisoners passed a handful of philosophers standing on steps along the route, imploring local people not to sully themselves by surrendering to the uncivilized barbarity of the Roman appetite for displays of violence. Few people paid any attention to them.

Outside the city gate a sea of people stretched down to the vast wooden structure constructed to stage the governor's spectacle. Masts rose up around the oval with bright red banners that wafted out in the light breeze. The holding cages for the condemned prisoners were beneath the seating under the arena. There were more cages for the animals that had been bought to take part in the entertainment and as Marcus and the others were thrust into their new prison they could hear the roar of bears, with the barks and howls of dogs, above the din of the crowd. Festus and Lupus eased Marcus down against the iron bars of the cage and the bodyguard conducted a brief examination of its structure but there were no weak points and he slumped down beside the boys in frustration.

The cage was twice the size of the cell at the palace but just as uncomfortable in its own way. Above them the timber framework of the supports stretched up and then there were the raked rows of seating, and dust kept dropping down from above as the stands filled up. There was little air movement beneath the arena and the stench of the animals, mingled with the human waste of the prisoners made the air foetid and unpleasant to breathe. There was one slight advantage, though. A gap beneath the lowest tier of seating provided a limited view of the arena and by standing up in the cage the prisoners could follow proceedings.

Around the cages, crammed beneath the seating, were many of the props and piles of equipment to be used in the spectacle. Aside from the gladiator fights scheduled for the last three days as the high point of the show, there were acrobats, comedy mime shows, animal hunts, beast fights, boxing and wrestling, as well as the public execution of criminals. As Marcus recalled from his days in Rome, the latter usually took place at noon when the audience settled down for their midday snack.

His head cleared as the morning wore on and he touched the side of his skull where the soldier had hit him, wincing at the tenderness of the bruised area.

'You're a real sight,' Festus mused. 'Looks like your face was hit with a hammer.'

'That's what it feels like,' Marcus replied. 'But other than that I'm all right.'

'So what happened? They brought you back unconscious. You stirred a bit during the night and yelled that you would choke the life out of Decimus, then went out again. Can you remember what happened?'

Marcus concentrated and it all flooded back in a rush of images and emotions. He forced himself to organize his thoughts and explained to the others what had happened.

'I thought it might be Euraeus,' said Festus. 'I didn't trust him from the outset.'

Lupus shot him a withering look. 'Bit late to say that now.'

Festus shrugged. 'It was very neatly worked. You have to hand it to Decimus, he runs a competent organization. It's a damned shame that he was working against Caesar. We could have made good use of him back in Rome.'

Marcus was surprised. 'You seem to admire him.'

'Why not? Just because he is my enemy does not mean I can't appreciate his abilities. Politics, business, the arena – it all boils down to the same thing in the end. Either you become good at your trade, or you get crushed by someone else. All the same,' he reflected, 'it's a damned shame that you didn't kill him last night when you had the chance, Marcus.'

'I tried, believe me. Maybe next time . . .'

Festus let out a deep laugh as he clapped Marcus on the shoulder. 'That's the spirit! Never say die.'

'Except that we are going to die,' Lupus interrupted bitterly as he thrust his hand out and pointed through the gap. 'Right there in the arena. And there's nothing that can be done about it. They're going to drag me across the sand and tie me to a post and then wild animals are going to maul me. They're going to rip me to shreds . . . shreds . . .' His face screwed up and he clenched his lips together tightly as he tried not to cry. Marcus could only watch, not knowing how to comfort his friend. What comfort was there? Everything that Lupus said was true. It was Festus who broke the awkward tension in the end. He cleared his throat.

'Lupus. I won't lie to you. That is almost certainly going to happen. I'm not saying that there is absolutely no chance of us being saved . . .'

Lupus shook his head. 'Don't! Don't say it. I don't want any false hopes.'

'Very well.' Festus chewed his lip as he made an awkward decision. 'If you can't face what's coming, then there is another way.'

Marcus frowned. 'Another way?'

Festus nodded. 'We don't have to die out there in the arena. We still have the choice in how we die. We have that at least.'

Marcus understood at once. But he shook his head. 'That's not for me.'

'It doesn't have to be you. I can do it for you, and Lupus. I can make it quick and relatively painless. Then I can see to myself.'

'What?' Lupus stared at the bodyguard as if he were mad. 'You're offering to kill Marcus and me?'

'Kill? Yes. But at least you would be spared what the governor has in mind for you.'

Lupus shook his head and backed away, holding his hands out. 'No. No. Stay away from me.'

Festus could not hide his anguish any longer. 'Listen, boy! Have you ever seen how a man dies when he's been condemned to the beasts?'

Lupus shook his head.

'It's a bad death, Lupus. One of the worst. You need to know that. Do you think I make this offer easily?' His voice caught as he tried to contain his emotion. 'You two boys are the closest thing I have to family. It would break my heart to see you suffer a cruel death in the arena. A humiliating death. I can give you a different ending. But it's your choice. It has to be. Think it over. If that's what you want then I can help you. If not, then say nothing and I won't mention it again. We'll face what comes together.'

Before Lupus could respond there was a shrill blare of trumpets and the crowd let out a great roar as they drummed their feet. To the ears of those held in the cages, the sound was deafening.

'It's beginning!' Festus cupped a hand and shouted to be heard above the din. They lined the side of the cage nearest the sand of the arena and stared out through the gap. Gradually the crowd quietened down and there was near silence before a voice rang out. Marcus recognized it at once: Euraeus.

'Citizens of Athens! Romans! Honoured travellers from further afield, you are welcome to this great event in the name of Governor Caius Servillus and the people of Rome. For the next five days you will witness one of the greatest spectacles ever to be provided in these lands. You will bear witness to the best entertainment in the known world! For years to come, when people hear you talk of the spectacle provided by his excellency, Caius Servillus, they will curse themselves that they were not here to share the experience, to share the privilege of seeing the finest gladiators compete for the title of champion of the games. You will count yourselves blessed that you were here. That you saw it with your own eyes. Heard it with your own ears. Felt it with your own heart! Without more ado . . . Let the games begin!'

The crowd let out another roar and pounded their feet on the boards beneath their seating, and Marcus wondered if the arena might collapse under the barrage of boots. But it held up and the trumpets sounded again as the priests emerged from an entrance on the far side of the arena, three austere figures in hooded white gowns. Behind them came several junior priests carrying a small brazier, which was already alight, while others led the sacrificial goat, its white hide gleaming brightly as it bleated anxiously.

The priests raised their arms in a quick supplication to the gods before their leader drew a knife and cut the throat of the goat. It kicked with all its strength as it bled out on the sand and then lay still. The priest cut open its chest and removed its heart, then examined it closely. An expectant hush fell over the crowd until the priest raised his head and announced that the omens were favourable. The Gods had blessed the games and the event could continue. There was more cheering as the priest tossed the heart into the flames of the brazier so that they could consume the heart and let the smoke carry the offering up to the Gods.

'Well, there's a surprise,' Festus commented wryly. 'Good omens. Fancy that.'

Marcus looked at him. 'Have you ever known the omens to be unfavourable?'

'What do you think? No. Not ever.'

After the priests had left the arena there followed a procession of the main performers, with the gladiators in gleaming ceremonial armour as they waved a greeting to their fans in the crowd. They were followed by carts filled with loaves of bread, pastries and honeyed cakes that slaves tossed into the crowd. By the time the first act came on, a troupe of acrobats, Marcus had lost interest and sat back on the straw to rest. The others joined him but there was little conversation. There was nothing to be said and they sat in silence, wrapped up in their own thoughts.

Towards the end of the day some guards brought several more condemned prisoners to join them. Six men and a woman, all of them convicted of murder. The oldest of them, a tall thickset man, stood over Festus and the boys with his hands on his hips.

'The name is Epatus. Everyone in Athens knows me.'

'We're not from Athens,' Festus replied. 'Never heard of you.'

Epatus frowned. 'Well, you have now. I've been condemned to be burned. You know the routine. If I subject to having my arm burned to a crisp without crying out in pain then I get pardoned. If I whine, then the rest of me gets roasted. Same for the others.' He jerked his thumb at those who had been put into the cage along with him. 'Except the woman. She's been condemned to the beasts. Poor bloody cow.'

Festus smiled grimly. 'Then it looks like me and the boys will have some company.'

Epatus puffed his cheeks. 'That's bad luck, that is.'

'Friend, in our situation, none of us is exactly having any good luck.'

Epatus laughed and sat beside Festus. 'I was going to sling you off the straw for the night, but you're a good sort.' He thrust out his hand and after a moment's hesitation Festus clasped his arm. 'I'm Festus, and these here are Marcus and Lupus.'

The Athenian cocked an eyebrow. 'Oh, I've heard about you. Murdered that slave auctioneer up in Stratos.'

'Not murder,' said Marcus. 'It was an accident. We're not murderers.'

'Small world,' Epatus grinned. 'Same with me and the rest of us. Shameful miscarriage of justice I call it. But then anyone in his right mind would. The Gods will play their little games with us.' He eased himself back and crossed his arms behind his head. 'Now, if you don't mind, I'm going to rest. Want to look fresh for my performance tomorrow.' He winked, then closed his eyes and shifted until he was comfortable.

'Takes all sorts,' Festus muttered. 'But he's right. Try and sleep, boys. If you can.'

After the day's events had ended, some guards came late in the evening with a pail of cold stew that had set into a glutinous mess. Only Epatus and a few of the men had any appetite for it. The rest sat in silence except for the dumpy middle-aged woman who, Epatus explained, had killed her husband in his sleep after years of being beaten by him every time he came home drunk. She sat slumped in the corner, weeping and muttering to herself about who would care for her children after she was gone.

As the moon rose over the city the noises around them died away, save for the howl of a dog until one of the arena staff went into its cage and beat it into silence. Marcus was awake through the long hours of the night, his thoughts drifting aimlessly from memory to memory, with a few bitter regrets thrown in. He wanted to believe that he had done all he could to save his mother and hoped that if she ever discovered his fate, then she would understand that he had died trying to save her.

At the same time his heart was heavy with the knowledge that he was responsible for the situation he and his two friends were facing. If he had listened to Festus and thought twice about approaching the governor then they would not have been arrested. Looking up, he saw Festus sitting with his arms resting on his knees as he stared blankly ahead. He had every right to be bitterly angry with Marcus. Yet Festus had treated him like a father, disappointed with an errant son, rather than being angry. Marcus smiled sadly to himself as he realized that behind the hard exterior Festus presented to the world, he had a heart after all. It was only then that Marcus grasped how fond he had grown of the man who had trained, advised and protected him from the day he had joined Caesar's household. He had let Festus down with his poor judgement, and worse, he had never told him the truth about his real father. A painful surge of guilt filled his heart and he hurriedly cuffed away the tears that were pricking his eyes.

When dawn came the crowds returned to the arena and the morning's entertainment began with beast fights. Festus watched for a while, admiring the technique of some of the beast fighters and tutting at the sloppy work of the others. Most left the arena unscathed but a bear managed to kill two men before it in turn was cut down. There was one more event, when a fresh bear was taken out and chained to a stake before being attacked by a pack of dogs. The crowd, following tradition, cheered the lone bear as it twisted and swiped at its tormenters. In the end the last of the dogs was killed and the bear was led out, roaring with pained defiance as the crowd gave it a cheer.

The door of the cage rattled and Marcus looked up to see several burly men outside. Their leader was muscular with a scarred face, and a whip hung from a loop on his belt.

'Murderers of Pindarus, on your feet!'

Marcus and Festus stood up as calmly as they could. Lupus edged away towards the back of the cage, his lips trembling. Marcus stood in front of him and spoke gently. 'There's nothing we can do about it, my dear friend. They have come for us. All that remains is to go with dignity. Come.' He held out his hand. Lupus stared at it a moment before he grasped it. Marcus felt his friend's flesh trembling as he helped him to his feet, but kept hold of his hand. Festus smiled at them and turned to lead them out of the cage.

'May the Gods deliver a quick end!' Epatus called after them.

The leader of the arena staff and his men marched them under the seating to the nearest gate leading on to the sand. Several stout posts were leaning against the side wall. The man pointed to them. 'Off with your tunics and then pick up one of those each. Move it!'

They did as they were told, slipping out of their tunics and standing in their loin cloths. Once they had picked up their stakes and rested them across their shoulders the man peered out through a crack in between the doors, then he turned round. 'Right, they're ready for us. You're on.'

He thrust the gates open and Marcus blinked as the dazzling

sunlight flooded the entrance. He felt a hand push him roughly forward and he stumbled into the arena. As his eyes grew accustomed to the light he saw the sea of faces rising up on all sides, the hubbub of their conversation like a distant storm. There were dark stains on the sand and the heat of the sun reflected off the white sand, beating at Marcus's exposed skin. Together with their escort they marched solemnly across the sand towards the box where the governor and his guests sat on cushioned chairs in the shade of an awning. Marcus could see the governor sharing a joke with one of his companions and he felt a seething, impotent rage as he saw that it was Decimus.

'This'll do,' the arena official decided. 'Down stakes.'

Marcus heaved his burden from his shoulder and let it drop on to the sand. He was dimly aware of Festus and Lupus on either side of him, but his attention was fixed on Decimus. The crew erected the stakes and drove them down into the sand using heavy mallets. When the official was satisfied that they would not budge he gave the order to tie the prisoners. Rough hands thrust Marcus back against the stake and he felt the wood smack against his spine. His hands were drawn back and tied at the wrists with leather thongs. More thongs bound his ankles to the stake and his waist and neck so that he could barely move.

When all three had been prepared the official strode behind each of them to test the bindings. Marcus was last, and he felt the breath of the man as he leaned his head to inspect the thongs. He paused and Marcus felt a hand on his shoulder, where he had been branded as an infant with the secret mark of Spartacus.

'What's this?' the official whispered. 'Speak up, boy. Where did you get this mark?'

Marcus swallowed and replied defiantly. 'From my father.'

'Your father . . .' the official wondered aloud. 'I know this mark . . . I know it.'

'Are you quite finished, man?' Euraeus called out from the governor's box.

The official straightened up. 'Yes, sir. Nearly done.'

'Then get on with it.'

The official moved round to face Marcus with a strange expression on his face. Then he turned and gestured to one of his men who was holding a bucket with a ladle. The man approached and took out the ladle, containing a dark red gloop, and threw it over Lupus's chest.

'Urghh!' Lupus flinched and wrinkled his nose in disgust.

The man threw another ladle over his stomach and then did the same for Marcus and Festus. The stink of the blood and offal caught in Marcus's throat as the man stepped back with a cold smile of satisfaction.

'There. That'll whet the beasts' appetite nicely!'

The official in charge took a last look at Marcus before he waved his staff towards the entrance. 'Let's go! At the double!'

They ran across the sand and hurriedly closed the gate behind them. On the other side of the arena another member of the arena staff climbed over the opposite gate and began to wind it up.

'What will it be?' Lupus whimpered. 'Bears? Wolves? Lions?'

'Not lions,' Festus replied. 'Only Rome has the right to use lions.'

Marcus could see the paws of the animals that would be used to kill them beneath the bottom of the gate as it began to rise. An instant later there were other shapes there. Muzzles, the glint of bared teeth and furry bodies. With a squeal the gate continued to wind up and the first of the beasts squirmed through and bounded a short distance on to the sand.

Marcus swallowed. 'Wild dogs then . . .'

18

Several dogs emerged from the holding cell behind the gate; large, shaggy beasts with slavering jaws. They looked around the arena and up at the crowds that bayed for the blood of the three prisoners tied to stakes in front of the governor's box. The noise and the seething movement of the crowd agitated them and the dogs snarled and snapped, lips curling up to reveal yellowy white fangs. Marcus felt his blood go cold at the sight and to his side he heard Lupus muttering.

'The Gods save me . . . Gods save me . . .'

Glancing at Lupus Marcus saw that his friend's eyes were wide with terror as he writhed against the leather straps that bound him to the wooden post. His efforts were futile and his muscles strained as he gritted his teeth and struggled. Looking quickly the other way, Marcus saw that Festus stood stiffly, his face a mask of defiant contempt. Yet there was a telltale tremor in his cheek that revealed the fear that the bodyguard was fighting to conceal in his determination to die with as much dignity as the circumstances allowed. But Marcus could not imagine any dignity in a death that involved being torn apart by a pack of wild, half-starved dogs. There was only shame in that, given an edge by the prospect of the sick amusement it would provide to the mob. It would have been better to accept the mercy killing offered to them by Festus, but it was too late for that.

He turned his face back towards the dogs, no more than thirty paces away. Their initial nervousness at their surroundings had passed and now they had caught the scent of the blood and offal daubed down the fronts of Marcus and his friends. Heads down and fangs bared, they spread out and approached, pausing every few paces to sniff the air. One of the dogs was bigger than the rest with a huge head and a scar above one eye, which had left the skin bare around it. The animal seemed to be the pack leader, as it remained a short distance in front of the other dogs and they did not dare move ahead of it.

Marcus could understand why. It looked ferocious and had the body of a hunting dog – large, lean and powerful. Half of one ear seemed to have been bitten off and a thick leather collar with short iron spikes hung round its neck. Marcus guessed that it must have been used in fights with other animals before it had joined the beasts chosen for Governor Servillus's games. It stopped when it was ten paces from its intended victims and raised its muzzle into the air, nose twitching. Another dog, thickset and dark, brushed past it, eyes fixed on Marcus as it crept forward. The large dog snarled and its companion flinched and dropped to its belly, small dagger-like ears swept back as it growled but did not quite dare to defy the larger animal. The rest of the dogs edged forward on each side, closing the gap towards the three stakes.

The hunting dog sniffed again, then slowly turned its head towards Marcus and fixed its dark brown eyes on him, unblinking. He felt a cold dread seize his limbs and bit his lip to stop himself crying out in terror. Marcus did not want to die screaming in agony as the jaws of the dogs tore at his flesh. But the thought of it, the dread of the moment when they began to maul him, filled his mind and the strength drained so abruptly from his legs that he would have collapsed had he not been tightly tied to the post.

Lupus was still calling out to the Gods for mercy, his voice growing louder and more shrill each time. Festus glared at the dogs and spoke in an undertone.

'Go on then, you brutes! Get on with it!'

With a soft growl the hunting dog approached Marcus, warily pacing towards the helpless boy as it continued to sniff, tilting its head slightly one way, then the other. Marcus closed his eyes tightly, blocking out the vision of the brute, but even above the roars of the crowd he was certain he could hear the faint rustle of its breath. He prayed to the Gods that the animal would tear out his throat so that he could bleed to death quickly and be spared the horror of being eaten alive. Every muscle in his body was now tense, every inch of his skin tingling with terrified anticipation.

'No . . .' he heard Lupus whimper.

'Don't show any fear,' said Festus. 'Let 'em see how Romans die.'

Marcus felt a soft nudge of fur against his thigh and he lurched against his bonds, unable to prevent a panicked cry. Then he felt the warm rasp of the hunting dog's tongue and a quiet, plaintive whine. It was too much to bear and Marcus opened his eyes and stared down at the scarred head of the dog. He was about to shout at the animal when he stopped. There was no bloodlust in the beast's eyes, no hint of violence at all, just an adoring gleam. The dog licked him again and rubbed its head against his legs, and Marcus felt a shocking sense of disbelief as he stared into its eyes and whispered.

'Cerberus . . .'

At the mention of its name the hunting dog wagged its long tail and rose up on its hind legs, pressing its paws on Marcus's shoulders as it licked his face, an urgent whining sound in its throat.

'Cerberus.' Marcus smiled, memories of the years he had spent with the dog tumbling back. 'Enough, boy. Down.'

But the animal's joy was too great for it to be told what to do now. When it finished with his face it began to lap at the offal and the sensation tickled Marcus so that he laughed out loud. A warm flow of relief swept through his veins. His limbs still trembled, but from shock this time. Around them the arena was growing quiet and still as the crowd looked on in disbelief. Marcus was unaware of them as his heart filled with love for his pet, and grief for what had become of it. He had thought Cerberus was gone, beaten to death by the men who had killed Titus and kidnapped Marcus and his mother. He must have lived, and been found by a new owner, one who saw Cerberus's size and strength as an excuse to use the animal for fighting. Marcus could only guess at the cruelties his dog had been subjected to.

His thoughts were interrupted by Festus. 'Marcus, the dog knows you! How is that possible?'

'He's mine.' Marcus choked back his tears. 'My dog, my friend. From childhood.'

'Well, I pray that his loyalty to you is greater than his loyalty to his pack.'

Marcus looked past the shaggy head of Cerberus and saw that the other dogs were edging forward, intent on carrying out the task given to them. The black dog with narrow ears was only a few paces from Marcus and he could see the savage glint in its eyes. It braced its legs ready to spring.

'No!' Marcus cried out, too late. The dog bounded forward a step and leapt at his throat. Cerberus turned to see the danger and jumped into its path, and the dogs collided with a soft thud, rolling on the ground in a blur of paws, fur, sand and teeth. Cerberus scrambled to his feet, head down and jaws locked in a throaty snarl as his hair rose along his spine. The black dog hunched low, six feet away, fangs bared as it growled and then barked. Marcus watched them facing off, filled with hope that Cerberus might save him, and fear that the animal would be hurt.

Then the other dog pounced. Cerberus lurched to one side and twisted as his opponent landed on the sand. He jumped, crushing the dog down with his paws, and buried his jaws in the short fur of its neck. The animal let out a yelp of pain and struggled to free itself, jerking violently from side to side. It tore free and rolled back on to its feet, crouching, as blood dripped from its dark fur on to the white sand. Most of the other dogs had backed off, but two were edging round the fight towards Lupus. As he saw them he screamed.

'Get back! Back you filthy curs!'

Cerberus saw them at the same time and turned towards them and barked loudly, and they recoiled as if they had been struck. It took only an instant but his opponent took advantage of the diversion to spring back into the attack. In a blurred rush he leapt at the hunting dog, clamping heavy jaws into Cerberus's matted flank as he shook his head from side to side. Marcus felt his heart lurch as his dog let out a shrill yelp of pain and tried to wrench itself free, but the black dog hung on, working its jaws. With a powerful thrust, Cerberus forced the other dog back until it fell. The impact loosed its grip and Cerberus pulled free then lunged at one of its paws and closed his powerful jaws with a sharp crunch of flesh and muscle. The black dog let out a piercing howl as the hunting dog worried the crushed limb for a while longer before releasing it and backing away. Ears folded flat, his defeated opponent slunk away, limping and bleeding.

'That's my Cerberus!' Marcus shouted gleefully. 'Well done, boy! Well done.'

But there was no time for anything more as the dogs that had moved on Lupus were advancing again. Their hunger drove them forward, despite the warning of their pack leader, and Marcus could only watch helplessly. Lupus cried out in terror and Cerberus's head turned towards him as he leapt forward, crashing into the side of the nearest dog, a powerfully built hound with a tan hide, and knocking him flying. Another dog managed to swerve round the tangle of furry limbs and raced straight for Lupus. As it made to leap at his offal-stained chest, something struck it in the side and it instinctively spun round to look.

Marcus saw a broken clay cup lying on the sand. Someone must have thrown it from the crowd. Glancing up, he saw people cheering excitedly at the unexpected turn of events. No one had seen an execution of criminals turn out like this before and they were cheering for Cerberus as he fought to protect the humans.

'Come on, boy!' Marcus shouted out. 'Come on, Cerberus!'

'Cerberus!' Festus bellowed. 'Cerberus!'

Marcus heard the cry repeated in the crowd as it spread quickly.

'That's it!' Festus cried out excitedly. 'Keep 'em at it! Cerberus!'

The large hunting dog bit into the head of the tan dog and tore at its ear. Drops of blood flicked through the air as the animal pulled free, leaving a gaping tear in fur and flesh at the top of its head. Cerberus growled as it retreated and then turned his head from side to side, daring the rest of the pack to take him on, or try to get past him to Marcus and the others. For a moment it seemed as if he had them cowed but another hunting dog stepped forward, dark hackles up as it growled. It had only one eye, the left socket empty and crudely stitched up. The remaining eye fixed on Cerberus and it stopped a short distance from him as it lowered itself into a crouch. Cerberus snarled and stood foursquare, as if trying to intimidate his new challenger by his greater height. If that was the intention, it didn't work. The one-eyed rival shuffled forward and then leapt. Cerberus reacted a fraction too slowly and tried to counter-attack with a charge of his own. The momentum was with the other hunting dog and it knocked Cerberus on to his back and fell on him, snapping with its jaws as its claws scrabbled furiously against its opponent's chest.

The crowd let out a gasp of dismay and leaned forward before someone called the dog's name again, and others joined in. Marcus could only look on helplessly as the two beasts snapped and clawed at each other in a savage blur of teeth and fur, as blood flecked the sand around them. Try as he might, Marcus's dog could not break free of his opponent and was pinned down under his weight. Marcus could see that Cerberus had several wounds already and he felt a surge of despair as he saw the animal's suffering.

'Get up, Cerberus!' he cried out as hot tears filled his eyes. 'Don't give in, boy!'

With a quick twist of his back, Cerberus freed his hind legs up and braced them against the belly of the other dog, then began to scratch and kick, tearing into the thin layer of fur covering his stomach. The one-eyed dog reared up then caught a kick in the chest and tumbled on to his side. At once he scrambled back up and met Cerberus head on, both dogs rising on their hind legs as they bit at each other and lashed out with their claws.

'Cerberus! Cerberus!' the crowd cheered.

The one-eyed dog suddenly tilted its head to strike at its rival's throat. Cerberus struck first, lunging forward and biting hard into the windpipe of the other dog. It tried to growl but the sound was muffled by the pressure on its neck and it twisted desperately from side to side as Cerberus hung on grimly, worrying away. Slowly the other dog began to weaken and its movements became feeble until it collapsed on the ground. Cerberus kept his grip, using one paw to press down on the writhing flank of the one-eyed dog. All the time the crowd's cheering increased in volume and hysteria. At last the loser went limp and lay on its side in the sand. Cerberus slowly released his grip then stood over his victim to make sure it was finished. Marcus took a deep breath and closed his eyes in relief.

When he opened them he saw the arena official and his men running across the sand carrying staves. They shouted and waved at the dogs, driving them away from Marcus and the others. Only Cerberus remained, feet planted apart as he stood in front of Marcus and snarled.

'Easy boy,' Marcus said comfortingly, fearing for his dog's safety as the official and two of his men approached. 'Easy. Don't hurt them.'

Cerberus looked round and cocked his head to one side, as if unsure. Then he turned and sat at Marcus's feet and thrust his big, furry head against Marcus's hip as he wagged his tail.

'What's going on?' Lupus asked, bewildered.

Around them everyone in the arena had risen to their feet, waving strips of cloth in the air to indicate that they wanted the prisoners spared. Looking up at the governor, Marcus could see that Servillus was anxiously conferring with his advisors.

'It's over!' Festus exclaimed. 'The crowd want us to live. The governor won't dare to refuse them. We're spared!'

'Spared?' Lupus shook his head then started shaking.

The official stepped warily round Marcus and took out his knife. Cerberus raised his head and growled.

'Better keep that dog under control, if you don't want it hurt,' the official threatened.

Marcus nodded to him and spoke to Cerberus. 'Easy, boy. Sit there, nice and quiet.'

Behind him he felt the man cutting his bonds. First his feet came free, then his hands, waist and lastly his neck. He stumbled forward the moment the rope parted and slumped to his knees as he threw his arms round Cerberus. 'Good boy . . . Good boy,' he murmured. 'I've missed you . . . How I've missed you.'

Marcus laughed with joy as he felt the wet nose thrusting towards his cheek and a warm tongue slathered his skin. Then he felt a hand on his shoulder and glanced up to see Festus grinning down at him.

'Care to introduce me to your fierce canine friend?'

Marcus patted the dog's head. 'This is Cerberus.'

'I guessed that part.'

Marcus smiled. 'He's mine. Or was, back when I lived on the farm.'

'Seems he still is your dog. Thank the Gods.'

Marcus looked round and saw Lupus sitting in the sand

hugging his knees as his shoulders heaved. Beyond, the crowd stood waving strips of cloth in delirious celebration of the extraordinary event that had just taken place.

'Heads up! Here comes his nibs,' the official called to the two men who had cut the prisoners free. The others had rounded up the dogs and driven them back into the holding pen. Striding across the sand towards the stakes was Governor Servillus, a small entourage of companions behind him. Marcus's smile faded as he saw Decimus scowling at him over the governor's shoulder.

'Astonishing!' The governor beamed as he stopped a safe distance from Marcus and Cerberus. 'Quite the most astonishing thing I have ever seen. Those dogs were supposed to rip you to pieces. They've been trained to do it and starved and beaten to make them savage. This beast most of all. Now look at him! Just like a little puppy. How on earth did you do it, boy?'

'He's my dog, sir,' Marcus explained. 'We were parted two years ago when I was kidnapped. Cerberus was clubbed to the ground by the men who did it. I thought he was dead all this time.' He looked down and stroked Cerberus's good ear and the dog lifted his nose and half closed his eyes in bliss as his nostrils flared.

Servillus shook his head in wonder. 'Quite a story. It's almost as if the Gods have had a hand in this. Well, I'm not one to intervene when the Gods have made their will so obvious. It's clear to me that the two of you were meant to be reunited.'

The governor turned to the crowd and raised his hands to command silence. Gradually the cheering subsided and the people sat in quiet expectation as Servillus addressed them.

'People of Athens! I had hoped to put on a show that would be remembered for years to come. Today my hopes have been rewarded! I have never seen the like of what we have just witnessed! I give you the champion of the day's games. Cerberus!'

The crowd roared their approval and the governor spoke again.

'I order that the master of Cerberus, and his companions, are set free. Free to leave the arena!'

The crowd cheered again and people waved their strips of cloth as Decimus bustled forward to join the governor, his expression black and angry.

'These men are condemned for murder, your excellency. Are you going to allow them to walk free?'

Servillus turned to him. 'Look at the crowd, Decimus. They love this dog and the boy. Are you prepared to defy their wishes? I know I'm not.'

'The mob is fickle, noble Servillus. Continue with the execution. Bring on some other animals and send this miserable wretch of a hunting dog back to his cage. Once the blood flows the crowd will forget soon enough.'

'Actually, I'm trying to avoid bloodshed. One thing a wise man learns is never to go against the will of the people if it can be avoided. That is why I am governor of this province and you are not, Decimus. Now please take your place, back with the others, and let me deal with this.'

Decimus flashed a bitter glance at Marcus, but he gave way and paced back towards the governor's entourage.

Servillus turned to Marcus. 'Stand up, boy. Acknowledge the crowd. It's the least you can do after they have compelled me to favour you and your friends.'

Marcus rose and looked round the arena, then punched his fist into the air, and the spectators erupted with another cheer.

Servillus kept a smile on his face as he stood beside Marcus and rested a hand on his shoulder.

'Does this mean we are free, sir?' Marcus asked quietly. 'To do as we will?'

Servillus shot him a warning glance. 'Take your victory, boy, while you can. You re free to leave the arena. I suggest that you leave Athens and return to Rome, before you get in any more trouble.' He patted Marcus on the shoulder and turned to wave to the crowd one last time before heading back to the steps that led to his box. Festus and Lupus stood with Marcus and Cerberus as they acknowledged the wild cheers of the crowd. Then Marcus felt a nudge in his back as one of the arena staff muttered.

'That's your lot. You three better get moving. It's a tight programme and we've got other executions to come. Off you go, sharpish!'

The three made their way across the sand with Cerberus walking at Marcus's side. As they left the arena he glanced back and saw the woman who had shared their cell the previous night being dragged towards the stakes. Marcus tore his gaze away as Lupus spoke to him.

'By the Gods, it's a miracle! I thought it was all over. I was sure of it.' He shook his head in astonishment.

Festus clapped the scribe on the shoulder and laughed with relief before he turned to Marcus. 'What now?'

'Now?' Marcus's expression became determined. 'Now, we finish what we came here to do. We free my mother, and make sure that Decimus pays the price for all the suffering he has caused.'

19

'Are you sure that's his house?' asked Marcus as they stood in the shade of a market portico on the far side of the street.

'I'm certain. I followed his litter here and that's where he went in, once he had dismissed his escort.'

'He might have been visiting a friend.'

Lupus shook his head. 'The litter went down the side alley there, towards the slave quarters at the rear of the house. If he was visiting it would have stopped by the front door.'

Festus nodded. 'True. Then that's where he is, most likely.'

Around them hundreds of people were perusing the stalls and haggling with the merchants selling exotic cloth, spices and scents from the far east. Thanks to the expensive nature of the products, the market was in one of the more affluent areas of Athens. Marcus reflected that it was typical of Decimus to choose the wealthiest area for his house.

Festus was still staring at the entrance across the street. A guard sat on a stool outside the door. Behind him the door itself was sturdy and studded with iron nails. A heavy grille allowed the doorkeeper within to examine visitors before he opened the door. The house occupied the whole of the block on which it had been built with narrow alleys along the sides and rear of the property. The walls were too tall to scale and there would be little question that Decimus would be guarded within.

'The question is, what do we do now?' Festus wondered. 'We can't get in there easily.'

Marcus sighed with frustration. He was desperate to discover where Decimus was holding his mother. His impatience was pressing him constantly. Following their release from the arena, they had been escorted back to the cell and forced to remain there until the end of the day. Marcus had passed the time cleaning Cerberus's wounds and had demanded some food for the dog before his hunger caused him to bite someone. As night fell they were taken back to the room in the guest wing and told their possessions would be returned in the morning, once they had been fetched from the palace storerooms. They had been destined for auction, the fate of any valuables left behind by those condemned to death. Two guards had been placed on the door who refused to let them leave, except if they needed the latrine and even then they were only allowed to go one at a time, a guard keeping close watch over them until they returned to the room.

The restrictions had angered them all. But no explanation was given for the delay in granting them a release from the governor's custody. It was not until the following morning that Euraeus had arrived to announce they were free to leave.

Festus had glared at the Greek. 'You have a lot to answer for, my friend.'

Smiling easily, Euraeus had tilted his head as he spoke apologetically. 'I was only doing my humble duty, sir. Your arrival at the palace, coming at almost the same time as the news from Stratos, was most unfortunate. What else was a reasonable man to conclude? But innocent or guilty, the governor has decided to release you.'

'Why the delay?' asked Festus. 'Why wait until morning?'

The Greek shrugged. 'I'm sure the governor has his reasons.'

'The governor, or you?'

'I am merely the servant of the governor. I do as he pleases and do not question my orders.'

'Liar!' Marcus snapped. 'You are in the pay of Decimus. It is his orders that you carry out.'

He had stepped towards the Greek, fists balled, and Euraeus instinctively recoiled, a frightened expression on his thin face. The restraining hand that Festus placed on Marcus's shoulder had caused Cerberus to rise up and let out a low growl until Festus withdrew.

'Think, Marcus. Think. This creature is not worth getting into any further trouble over. We must concentrate on finding your mother. Nothing else matters right now.'

For a moment, the urge to strike the Greek down had burned in his veins, but Marcus knew his friend was right. He must not allow himself to become distracted. He had taken a deep breath and stepped away from Euraeus.

'Good lad,' Festus had said gently before turning his attention back to the Greek. 'We'll go, nice and peacefully. I take it we are no longer welcome to stay in the palace until we leave Athens?'

A look of surprise had flashed across Euraeus's face. 'I assume you are joking, sir? The governor does not like hosting murder suspects, even if they are the darlings of the mob. You will be escorted to the palace gates and you are forbidden from entering the complex again under any pretext.' Seeing the anger in Festus's expression, he had retreated into the corridor outside, gesturing to the two guards. 'Take these people, and their brute, to the main gate and see them out of the palace.'

'Yes, sir.' Nodding, one of the guards had grasped the handle of his sword as he curtly gestured to Festus and the others. 'You lot, out now! Let's go!'

They had been forced on to the street and Marcus realized they could not take Cerberus with them since his size and savage appearance would attract too much attention. So they had hurriedly found a small storeroom to rent for the night at the back of a seedy inn, where they left the dog tied to a post while they went with Lupus to the house of Decimus.

Now, Marcus turned to Festus. 'What we must do is get in there and force the truth out of Decimus. One way or another.'

Lupus shook his head. 'There isn't any way in except for that door, and another like it at the rear of the house.'

'We must go through one of the doors,' Marcus said pigheadedly. 'If you won't help me then I'll do it myself.'

Festus lowered his face towards Marcus. 'Calm down. No one said we wouldn't help you. But we have to do this carefully. The governor let us off the hook once, but I doubt he'll look too kindly on us causing any further problems. So we have to take it easy. Understand?'

Marcus closed his eyes tightly, fighting off his frustration. But he had learned the value of caution so he sighed and nodded.

'That's better,' Festus said. 'Now we have to think about the best way of getting at Decimus. Perhaps we wait until he comes out again and summons his litter. Follow him and see if we can get to him when there's a chance.'

'What chance?' asked Lupus. 'He has eight men on the litter, a guard leading the way, and two more following. We can't take them all on.'

Festus nodded. 'You're right. But if he leaves the litter, then the odds are cut down significantly. He might make for the baths, or do some shopping, or some business. If he does, that's when we can make our move. We deal with his guards and take him somewhere quiet for a little talk.'

Marcus smiled at the prospect, but Lupus shook his head. 'We don't know when, or if, he is going to leave his house. We could be stuck here for hours, days even. Now that he knows we're in Athens he's bound to be careful. And the longer we stand here waiting, the more suspicion we'll arouse.'

Marcus turned to him impatiently. 'Well, what do you think we should do? Give up?'

'Certainly not. There is a way that might get us through that door. But first I need my writing materials. Listen . . .'

Marcus was still keeping watch when Festus and Lupus returned two hours later. Festus was carrying a small bundle under his arm and he parted company with Lupus at the end of the street before coming over to Marcus.

'How's Cerberus coping?' Marcus asked at once, anxious that his dog had been alone for most of the day.

'Not happy, as you might imagine. Pining for you the moment we returned. And he didn't seem to take kindly to being tied to a post either. Won't be for much longer, though, if this works.' He jerked his thumb towards Lupus who was waiting at the corner of a building.

'Do you think it will?'

Festus shrugged. 'What choice have we got? I can't think of anything better. We must put our trust in Lupus and be ready to act. Speaking of which . . .' He carefully undid the bundle of material and, making sure that no one saw them, revealed two swords. Marcus slipped one out of the bundle and under his cloak, before Festus flipped the material over the remaining sword and held it under his arm.

'Ready?'

Marcus nodded.

'Then let's do it.' Festus turned towards Lupus and made a small gesture. Then he and Marcus threaded their way through the market until they had passed fifty paces beyond the house of Decimus. When he was satisfied they were far enough away Festus turned back towards the entrance of the house, with Marcus at his side. They began to walk casually along the street, while ahead Marcus could see Lupus detach himself from the corner of the building and walk steadily towards them.

Lupus felt his heart beating fast against the inside of his chest as he made his way towards the man sitting outside the door. He had changed into his best tunic and cleaned his boots and combed his hair so that he might pass for a member of the governor's household. He climbed the two steps leading to the porch. The watchman did not bother rising from his stool but leaned forward slightly to block Lupus off from the door.

'Yes?'

'I've come from the governor's palace,' Lupus explained. 'With an urgent message from Euraeus to Decimus.'

'Let's see it then.' The watchman held out his hand.

Lupus tried to calm his nerves as he reached into his haversack and brought out the sealed letter. The wax seal bore an impression of an eagle and there was a neat signature across the fold in the parchment. The watchman examined it briefly and Lupus prayed that the seal he had carved from soap and the forgery of the Greek's signature would look real enough to pass muster. The watchman stood up.

'All right, I'll see it gets to him.'

Lupus had been expecting this and spoke up. 'Euraeus said I was to pass the letter into the hands of Decimus in person.'

'Too bad. The master is not at home.'

Given that Decimus was lying low, Lupus had also expected this and had a response ready. 'Then my orders are to ensure the letter is given directly to the steward of the house.'

The watchman frowned. 'In person, eh?'

Lupus nodded. 'Those were my strict instructions. That, and it is vital the letter is delivered as soon as possible.'

As he spoke Lupus saw Festus and Marcus approaching out of the corner of his eye and knew that the timing of what happened next was critical. With a weary sigh the watchman stood up and rapped on the door. A moment later the grille opened and a face appeared.

'Open up,' the watchman instructed, with a nod towards Lupus. 'Messenger from the governor's palace. Delivery to the steward.'

The grille snapped shut and there was a scraping groan as the doorkeeper slid back the locking bolt. With a faint squeal from the hinges the door began to swing inwards.

'Now,' Festus snapped in a low voice. He charged up from the street, Marcus at his side, swords in their hands in the blink of an eye. The watchman just had time to look over his shoulder before they piled into him, knocking him back against the door, which struck the doorkeeper and sent him sprawling. Lupus rushed in after them. Behind them a few people turned towards the sudden commotion, but before they could react Lupus had closed the door. A handful of passers-by hesitated, then shrugged and continued along the road as if nothing had happened.

Inside the atrium of Decimus's house Festus had knocked the watchman out and pulled his body behind one of the benches by the door. Marcus had his boot on the doorkeeper's chest and held the point of his sword to the man's throat.

'Decimus,' Marcus growled. 'Where is he?'

The doorkeeper was an older man, with weathered skin and a thin band of grey hair round his wizened head. He held his hands up imploringly as he muttered incoherently.

'Quiet, or I'll cut your throat where you lie,' Marcus hissed at him. 'Now, I'll ask you again. Where is Decimus? Which room?'

'The M-master's not here!' the doorkeeper whimpered.

Marcus froze. 'Not here? Not in the house?'

The doorkeeper shook his head.

'Then where is he?'

'G-gone.'

Marcus gritted his teeth in frustration. They had kept a close watch on the house all day and Decimus had not gone out. Not by the front door anyway. He might have used the slave entrance but Marcus doubted it. A man of Decimus's lofty social station would not be able to stomach that.

'When did he go?'

'Yesterday. As soon as he returned from the g-games. He gave orders for his horses to be made ready and left as soon as they were saddled.'

Marcus withdrew his sword as his mind took in the news. Festus and Lupus came and stood round the prone doorkeeper whose rheumy eyes flitted from one to the other.

'I sw-swear it's true. He's not here.'

'Damn!' Festus balled his hand into a fist. 'That explains why we were held until this morning. Euraeus wanted to give Decimus a chance to leave Athens before we came looking for him.' He leaned over the doorkeeper. 'Where did Decimus go?'

'I-I-I . . .'

Marcus poked the point of his sword into the man's neck, pricking the skin so that a thin trickle of blood ran down his neck. 'You tell us! And you tell us the truth. You even think about lying and I'll cut your throat, right here and now!' He let the threat sink in before he continued in a cold deliberate voice. 'Where has Decimus gone?'

'To his estate . . . Close to Tegea. That's where you'll find the master. I swear it's true.'

'Tegea?' Marcus repeated, to be certain. The doorkeeper nodded. Marcus withdrew his sword and stood erect as he faced his friends.

'He's got a day's start on us. And he's on horseback,' Festus commented.

'Then there's no time to lose,' Marcus decided. 'We leave Athens at once and make for Tegea as fast as we can.'

The others nodded and Marcus swiftly prayed to Jupiter, best and greatest, that his mother would still be alive when they reached Tegea. If not, then he would not show one shred of mercy to Decimus.

20

They left Athens on foot, not having enough money to buy horses, and not willing to risk stealing any and being caught. They had won the governor's mercy once. There would be no second time. Festus calculated that it would take them three days to reach Tegea. Having gone through their packs, Festus stripped them down to the bare minimum for the coming march. They left behind all but their clothes, a cloak, canteens, hard rations and the weapons needed for the work at hand. All the rest was sold on the nearest market for a fraction of its true value.

Lupus had wanted to keep his writing case, but Festus had refused and the scribe could only look on in despair as a Greek merchant picked his way through the pens, inks, styli, waxed tablets and bundles of papyrus, pursing his lips with disdain before making a derisory offer. And Festus had accepted without argument. The only thing they bought was a short chain for Cerberus in case they needed to keep the dog on a lead.

There were still a few hours of daylight left when they quit the city and headed west at a fast pace set by Festus. They remained on the road that had brought them to Athens only a few days earlier and carried on marching as the sun dipped and sank behind the mountains, bathing the sky in changing colours as dusk stole across the landscape. Even as the last of the light faded and the stars began to prick out of the velvet darkness above, Festus kept up the pace and their boots crunched over the loose gravel on the road as the air around them swelled with the piercing sound of cicadas, rising and falling in a rhythm that only those small insects understood.

When they reached a junction where one branch led north and the other continued west to the Peloponnese, Festus stopped and led them a short distance off the road to the shelter of the nearest pine trees. They were already exhausted and did not bother with a fire, but just chewed on some dried meat. Marcus shared some of his rations with Cerberus and the dog hungrily chewed on them, finishing long before his human comrades. Then he settled to watch them eat in a pose of rapt concentration, in case any morsels slipped from their fingers.

Afterwards they built makeshift beds of pine branches over the carpet of fallen needles and curled up in their cloaks to sleep. The hunting dog lay on his side, pressing his furry back into Marcus and providing some welcome warmth.

Tired as he was, it still took Marcus a while to relax his mind and body. While the others slumbered, he stared through the branches above at the stars, tormented by thoughts of his mother and the desperate race to reach her before Decimus decided to do her any harm. He had a good lead and could reach his estate as much as two days ahead of them. Anything could happen in that time and Marcus dreaded the prospect of racing to the scene only to discover that his enemy had put an end to his mother.

As he briefly allowed himself to think that she might be dead, his mind filled with dark, bloody images of revenge. Decimus would die by his hand, which was all that would matter to Marcus. He had no thought of any life beyond that moment, only a dark, despairing void. So he tried to allow himself to hope. To imagine rescuing his mother, and seeing the love in her expression as he felt the comfort of her arms about him again. They would return to the farm, and Marcus would find a way to earn enough money to buy it back from whoever owned it now. In time they would build a proper tomb for Titus where his remains could be interred with due respect. They would work the land together and Cerberus would guard their sheep from the wolves during the winter. His mother would grow old but would never forget that Marcus had saved her, regarding him with pride and affection.

It was a pleasing world that his imagination had conjured up and it filled his heart with contentment, eventually allowing him to drift off to sleep. He did not wake even when Cerberus stirred in the middle of the night and sat bolt upright, nose sniffing the air and fixing on the sharp scent of a passing fox. He growled lightly and there was a rustling nearby as the feral animal turned and bounded off into the trees. Satisfied that his master was safe, the dog settled down and gave Marcus a gentle lick on his ear before lowering his head between his paws to fall into a blissful sleep.

Festus woke before dawn, just as the first rosy fingers of light reached over the horizon. He grimaced at the stiffness in his muscles as he sat up and stretched his shoulders and neck before standing to prod the sleeping forms of the two boys with his boot.

'Come on. Wake up!'

'Eurrgghh,' Lupus moaned, before turning away and curling

up in a tight ball. Festus muttered a curse and poked him again, harder this time.

'Get up, boy! Before I have to kick you.'

Lupus cursed him as he blinked his eyes open, rubbed them and eased himself up into a sitting position.

Marcus forced himself to stand and rubbed his eyes while Cerberus looked at them all in turn as he wagged his tail. Yesterday's fast pace had left Marcus's legs aching but he knew that worse was to come if they were to cover the distance to Tegea in the time that Festus had allowed.

'Eat something now,' the bodyguard ordered. 'I want to be on the road again at first light.'

Lupus sat still while his sleep-clouded mind gradually cleared. Then he reached for his haversack and took out another strip of the dried meat that Festus had bought in the market after selling the rest of their possessions. He stared at it with distaste.

'I hope we won't have to eat this all the time. Why don't we hunt hares like we did before, Festus?'

'Because we can't spare the time to hunt, build a fire and cook,' Festus replied tersely, then bit one end off the strip in his hand and began to chew. At length he continued, 'But we could buy some food on the way, if we get the chance.'

'We'll need to,' said Marcus as he handed one of the pieces to his dog. 'If only for Cerberus. He can't live on this.'

Festus nodded, looking at the dog, and then he finished chewing. 'It might have been better to leave him behind.'

Marcus looked up sharply. 'After he saved out lives? No. He stays with us. We may need him. Besides, at the moment, Cerberus is all that I have left to me from my family.'

'You have us. Not family as such,' Festus said awkwardly, 'but almost as close as family.'

Marcus stared at him and gave a light laugh of surprise. 'I never knew you cared.'

Festus scowled. 'What? You think we haven't known each other long enough to form a bond? And Lupus too. You think we'd have gone through all that we have just because Caesar told us to come with you? We're in this to the end, Marcus. Whether we find your mother and deal with that scum Decimus or not. That's what comrades do. Isn't that right, Lupus?'

The scribe was as startled by Festus's uncharacteristic outburst as Marcus. He nodded. 'Brothers in arms, and all that. Absolutely.'

Festus sighed. 'I was making a serious point.'

'And so was I.' Lupus smiled uncertainly.

There was a moment's awkward silence and Cerberus, with

that peculiar sense that dogs have for people's moods, looked to each of them in turn with big brown eyes full of concern.

'Right then!' Festus thrust his half-eaten strip of meat back in his shoulder bag and picked up his cloak. 'Enough of that emotional nonsense. Let's move. I want to reach Corinthos by the end of the day.'

The boys hurriedly made ready and joined the bodyguard as they hurried back to the road and set off. Festus set the pace, striding a few yards ahead. Lupus, thanks to his gangly height, kept up at first and Marcus came last, with Cerberus trotting at his side. He was still taken aback by their last brief exchange and he glanced down at the dog, raising his eyebrows as he whispered, 'Who would have thought it, eh, boy? Under that rock-hard skin, there is a very human heart after all.'

Cerberus looked up at the sound of his voice, then lifted his muzzle to sniff the cool morning breeze as he wagged his tail gently.

Marcus chuckled. 'Well, at least someone's happy.'

But Marcus's good humour did not last for many miles. Festus kept the pace up as they followed the road through terraced farms and past small whitewashed villages stirring into life as the sun rose into a clear sky. To their right the hills and mountains reared up, forested slopes a verdant green, while to their left the coast gave way to a blue sea, shimmering and sparkling in the morning sunlight. Mile after mile, the road wound along the coast and their feet began to ache long before noon when Festus finally called a halt beside a stream. The water was cool and refreshing and they soaked their feet in its soothing flow for a short while, before Marcus stood up to put his boots back on, the urgent need to reach Tegea weighing on his mind.

There were no more streams before they reached Corinthos at dusk and Marcus had to share the water in his canteen with Cerberus as they trudged beneath the beating afternoon sun. By the end of the day all their exposed skin was red and tingling from sunburn. But they were too tired to care and were asleep soon after collapsing on the cheap mattresses in a back room that they rented for the night from a dour innkeeper. They left before first light, limbs stiff and feet sore, and Lupus could only glance longingly at the dark outlines of the temples and theatres he would not have the chance to explore – at least not until their desperate hunt for Marcus's mother was over.

After they left Corinthos the road climbed into the mountains of the Peloponnese and the going became more difficult and exhausting. Even Cerberus, who had been enjoying the exercise of the previous days, now walked at Marcus's side with his long tongue hanging out as he panted. During the afternoon they came across a young shepherd who had killed some hares with his sling, and Festus bought four, which they cooked and ate that night. Except for one that Cerberus devoured raw, crunching contentedly on the bones as he sat in the glow of the fire.

'We'll reach Tegea tomorrow afternoon,' Festus announced as they finished their meal and made ready to sleep on the beds of pine branches at the edge of a forest, where Festus had decided to make camp.

'As Decimus has an estate close to the town, either he, or his servants, will soon get word that we've arrived. Decimus may even have instructed that he is to be informed the moment any man with two boys and a dog are sighted near Tegea. So we can't risk entering the town together. My plan is this. Marcus will enter Tegea alone while Lupus, Cerberus and I find somewhere to hide outside of the town. The moment you have located the estate, you come back and we scout it out together.'

'Scout it out?' Marcus frowned. 'We haven't time for that. The moment we know where the estate is, we must rescue my mother.'

Festus looked at him patiently. 'You're tired, Marcus. Your mind is troubled, and no wonder. But if we are to save your mother then we must give ourselves the best chance of doing it. We have no idea how many men guard the estate. We don't know where your mother is held. If you want to see her again, we must do this right. We go charging in there, swords out, then there's every chance we'll be killed, and there'll be no one to save her. Understand?'

Marcus felt himself torn between his heart and his head, but he knew that Festus was right. He forced his feelings to one side and nodded.

'Good. Then we'll get some sleep, after Lupus has done his sword exercises.'

The scribe groaned and shook his head. 'Not tonight. I'm shattered.'

'You may be shattered, lad, but you'll be dead if you don't know how to use a blade. Better get it right while you have the chance. It's more than likely you'll be fighting for your life very soon. Marcus, you sort him out. Don't go easy on him.'

'Why me?' asked Marcus. 'You're the one with training experience.'

'I'm also the one who's telling you to do it. Besides, you need something to take your mind off your worries. Now get to it, boys!'

They approached Tegea late the following afternoon and took a path leading off the road as soon as they came in sight of the town. They found a shallow cave below a cliff on the hills overlooking the town and downed packs while Festus gave his instructions, and some coins, to Marcus.

'Here, that's for some provisions. Buy us enough to get through the next two days. Make for the marketplace. If you want to find out where the estate is that's the best place to start asking. But be subtle. Last thing we want is to alert Decimus that someone is snooping around.'

'I know what to do,' Marcus replied firmly.

'Very well. Better tie Cerberus to a tree. We can't afford to have him track you down in the town. A dog like that will draw some attention to himself.'

A smile flickered across Marcus's face. With his large size and fierce appearance Cerberus would do more than draw attention. He'd frighten people. He took the chain they had bought in Athens from his pack and slipped the loop over the dog's head before tying the other end to the trunk of a tree. Cerberus thought it was a game and wagged his tail happily, until the moment that Marcus left the cave. Then the dog lurched towards its master and was drawn up swiftly at the end of his leash. He lowered his shaggy head and began to whine, but Marcus steeled himself against the sound as he started down the path towards Tegea.

★

The marketplace of Tegea was bathed in the red, ruddy glow of the sun and the colours of the cloth, fruit, vegetables and other wares for sale seemed to be ablaze in intensity. Marcus slowly passed between the food stalls, stopping every so often to examine the produce and listen in as discreetly as possible to conversations that sounded promising. Already many of the stallholders were packing up for the day so he hurried over to a baker and bought some bread, and then some dried fruit and cheese from another stall.

'That'll be . . . eight asses,' the trader concluded, holding out his hand.

Marcus reached into his purse to fish out the small bronze coins and paid them over. 'There.'

The trader took the coins with a nod of thanks and tucked them into his own purse as he glanced at Marcus. 'I know pretty much all my customers. Never seen you before.'

'I'm from Lerna,' Marcus replied casually, recalling the name of the small town they had passed earlier in the day. 'Or was. My father's sent me to look for work. Not enough land to support us all.'

The trader clicked his tongue. 'Hard times, lad.'

Marcus nodded. 'I don't suppose there are any large farms near Tegea that might need field hands? I'm a hard worker.'

The trader noted his powerful physique. 'Farm boy, eh? Well, there's only one place nearby that might take people on. If you don't mind working alongside chain gangs.'

'Oh, where's that then?'

'Up there.' The trader raised his hand and pointed up the slope of a large mountain outside the town, on the opposite side to the cave where Festus, Lupus and Cerberus were waiting. Marcus followed the direction he was indicating and saw a distant roof among some trees. As his eyes scanned the area he saw more buildings, and terraces of trees and vines.

'Looks like a big place.'

'Certainly is. One of the biggest estates in the Peloponnese. Mind you, that's what you'd expect given that it's owned by one of the biggest bloodsucking leeches in the whole of Greece. Squeezes us for every tax he can get his greedy hands on. That's why he's the only one who can afford to take on field hands. If you want some work, that's where I'd suggest you go. The estate of Decimus.'

21

'Seen anything new?' Festus asked as he crawled forward beneath the low boughs of the sapling and eased himself into place alongside Marcus. They were lying on a ledge, a short climb above the cave, which had a clear view of Decimus's estate. Lupus had taken the first watch, and was resting in the cave. Now Festus had made his way up to take over from Marcus.

Marcus consulted the waxed tablet he had borrowed from Lupus and glanced over the notes. 'The men on the gate were relieved at noon, the others shortly afterwards. Still the same number on watch.'

'Hmmm.' Festus strained his eyes and stared down at the villa. It was an elaborate affair, with an outer courtyard for visitors arriving on litters, in wagons or on horseback, with stables and shelters for slaves and servants waiting for their masters. A colonnade and arch led into the main courtyard, neatly divided in four by two wide paths that intersected round a fountain. Neatly kept hedges lined the paths and a profusion of flowers and shrubs were laid out in geometric patterns in each quarter of the courtyard. Another large colonnade ran round the garden and joined the main house, a sprawling two-storey structure facing south to make use of the natural light and warmth of the sun. There were two guards on each of the courtyard entrances and each of the small entrances at the rear of the main house, for the use of slaves and servants, was also guarded. A group of four men patrolled the grounds round the villa.

'Decimus won't be an easy man to reach,' Festus mused. 'Have you seen him yet?'

Marcus paused briefly. 'I think so. A man in a yellow tunic came out of the house earlier and walked round the garden. Same build and bald. If it's him, he doesn't seem to bother wearing a wig in the privacy of his own home.'

'That'll be him then.' Festus gave a slight smile before he turned to Marcus with a more serious expression. 'Any sign of your mother?'

Marcus shook his head. He gestured towards the line of trees a hundred paces from the villa. Beyond lay several long, low buildings with small slits to let in air and light – the barrack blocks of the slaves working on the estate. A wall surrounded the dismal-looking buildings and there was only one entrance, fortified by a tower on each side. At the moment the slaves were working in the fields, orchards and groves of the estate. Marcus had seen them emerge from the barrack first thing in the morning as he lay concealed close to the work camp. Gaunt figures in rags, chained in fours, stumbled into line and waited until the guards marched them through the gates to work. There had been plenty of women among them and some children, but Marcus had not been able to identify his mother.

'She may not be working in the fields,' Festus mused. 'Decimus might have placed her with the household slaves. It's possible, but unlikely. If she's a house slave then she won't be in chains. And if that's the case, from what you have said, I imagine she'd take every chance to try and escape. So I'd wager she's in with the field slaves. It won't be easy getting into the work camp to search each barrack block for her.'

Marcus thought the problem through. 'Then we find Decimus first. We get into the villa, track him down and force him to tell us where she is.' Marcus's eyes widened with excitement as he developed his idea. 'Better still, we get him to send for her. That way we don't risk going into the work camp.'

Festus sucked in a deep breath. 'Even assuming we can do that, we still have to get into the villa in the first place.'

'I think I know a way. It's time to put that Parthian bow of yours to work . . .'

The three of them waited until the moon was hidden by a passing cloud before they emerged from cover a short distance from Decimus's estate. It was close to midnight, as far as Marcus could calculate the passing of the last few hours as they lay in a ditch at the rear of the villa. The patrol had passed by shortly before and exchanged a brief greeting with the two men on the small gate leading into the slaves' quarters. Now they had turned the corner of the villa and were out of sight.

'Lupus, off you go,' Festus whispered.

After a moment's hesitation, the scribe summoned up his courage then rose into a crouch and headed away along the ditch. Festus reached for his bow case and nodded to Marcus as they eased themselves out of the ditch into the knee-high grass of the meadow that stretched up to the villa. They kept flat as they worked themselves close to the wall that gleamed dully in the moonlight. They had prepared for the night's action as best they could. Their faces were blackened with a paste made from charred wood and mud, and the same mixture had been rubbed into their tunics. Each of them wore a sword belt and carried daggers and throwing knives. Cerberus had been left at the cave with a marrowbone that Marcus had bought at the market to keep him busy. He would return for the dog when it was all over. If things did not work out as he wanted, then Marcus hoped that Cerberus would be found and looked after by a new owner.

They crawled steadily through the grass until they reached the woodpile beside the wall, twenty paces from the entrance to the slave quarters and the two guards. Then, hidden by the logs, they stood up. While Marcus kept watch Festus took out his bow and braced the tip against his boot, leaning into it as he strung the weapon. Once the loop of the drawstring had settled over the horn he eased his grip gradually until it was ready to use and took out three arrows from the case. Festus had decided to use hunting arrows with their big barbed heads so that the impact would stun the victim and the wound would bleed profusely. He fitted the first arrow and eased himself up, ready to strike, while they waited for Lupus to make his appearance.

One of the guards leaned against the wall while his companion stood rubbing the small of his back as his head tilted towards the heavens. All was still and Marcus began to wonder if Lupus had the courage to go through with their plan. Beside him, he could sense Festus's tense impatience as he stood ready to draw his bow. The guard let out a low groan as he stretched his back. Then he turned his face from the sky, and froze.

'Who's there?' he called out.

A figure had emerged from the shadows and was casually pacing along the wall towards the gate. A surge of relief flowed through Marcus and he heard the faint creak of the bow as Festus drew back his right arm.

'Is that you, Pythos?' The guard took a pace towards Lupus while his comrade pushed himself away from the wall and turned towards the person approaching. Marcus held his breath as Festus took aim. This was the most dangerous part of the plan. If Festus missed his target then the arrow might hit Lupus, even though he had moved out a short distance from the wall to get clear of Festus's line of sight.

There was a dull twang as the arms of the bow snapped forward and launched the hunting arrow towards the nearest of Decimus's men. It struck with a sharp whack, like a stick hitting a sheet of wet leather, and the guard pitched forward with a pained grunt to fall face first in the grass, groaning as he writhed feebly, struggling to reach behind his back for the arrow shaft. The other guard was still distracted by the approaching figure of Lupus, but the commotion behind caused him to turn and look back.

'Mantippus? You all right?'

He froze in shock, just long enough for Festus to draw his bow again, adjust his aim and loose his second arrow. The barbed head punched through his throat, severing blood vessels so that the guard could only claw helplessly at the shaft of the arrow. Blood filled his throat, mouth and lungs as he collapsed on to his knees with a horrible gurgling noise.

'Come on,' Festus commanded quietly, handing his bow to Marcus. They moved out from behind the logpile to join Lupus by the still moving bodies of the guards. 'Keep watch, lads. I've got some quick work to do here.'

While Marcus crouched down and kept his eyes fixed on one corner of the wall, Lupus did the same for the other end. Festus took out a heavy cosh hanging from his belt and struck each of the guards about the head so they lay unconscious as they bled out. Then he dragged the bodies to the entrance by the slave quarters. He propped the man he had shot in the throat against the wall and dumped the other behind the woodpile before turning to Lupus.

'You stay here. Stand by the gate. When the patrol comes round again they may call out to you. If it happens, then you'll have to say something. Keep it short and keep it quiet.'

'What if they come close enough to make me out?'

'It's dark, and they won't be close enough to see you properly.'

'If they do?'

'Then you'll have to make a run for it. Head for the cave. We'll meet there. Otherwise, we'll see you back here on the way out. Is that clear?'

Lupus nodded and Festus clapped him on the shoulder. 'Good lad. Right then, Marcus, boots off. We go as quietly as possible from here on in.'

They unlaced their boots and left them beside the door, then Festus muttered, 'Let's go.'

He lifted the latch on the door and eased it open before leading Marcus inside the villa. Marcus felt his heart pumping as they entered a small, gloomy yard surrounded by the doors to the slave quarters. He could hear snoring and some muttered conversation and he wondered briefly if his mother was there.

He touched Festus's arm and whispered, 'What if she's here? We should check this place first.'

'No. We can't risk it. We start waking people up, they'll make a noise and the rest of Decimus's thugs will be down on us like a ton of bricks. We stick to the plan. Come on.'

They made for a small arch on the far side of the slave quarters and entered a narrow service passage leading along the length of the private garden towards the rear of the main villa.

Marcus trembled as the walls pressed in on either side while ragged wreaths of cloud hid the stars above. At the end of the passage was a door leading into the kitchen, a large space with enough cooking hearths and large work tables for the villa's slaves to produce a banquet for their master and his guests. Storerooms were set off to one side and the air was filled with the smells of woodsmoke, roast meat and the heady aroma of spices.

A dim light burned in the far corner of the kitchen and Marcus saw a handful of figures sitting round a table on which a single oil lamp provided just enough illumination for them to see.

'They ain't ever going to bed at this rate,' one of the kitchen slaves muttered. 'Same as last night. Same as it's been since he got back from Athens. Him, and that man of his.'

'Aye, and that Thermon's a dark one,' another voice added. 'Right nasty-looking bugger. Sitting there, plotting with the master.'

'And he's looking scared, is Decimus,' the first voice responded. 'Never seen him so on edge. And he's taking it out on us. All of us, even his favourite.'

Marcus felt his blood stir at the mention of Thermon, but Festus plucked his tunic and they set off round the edge of the large room, keeping to the shadows as the slaves continued grumbling about being kept up to wait on their master. There was a heavy curtain over a doorway at the far end of the kitchen and they gently eased the material aside as they slipped out into a corridor beyond. Marcus heard the sound of more conversation ahead where a light glowed at the end. As they padded down the passage, Marcus could see that there was a large room ahead and the voices echoed off the high walls of the triclinium, the dining chamber of the villa. It was Decimus's voice that Marcus recognized first.

'You'll have to oversee the collection of taxes in Corinth for me.'

'Me?' a dry, deep voice replied. 'That ain't my speciality. Why not find someone else? Or better still, go yourself. The boys and I can keep you safe.'

'No. I'm staying here. Until it's over. We'll put a price on their heads, dead or alive. Big enough that there won't be a man in Greece who wouldn't stick a knife in their hearts to claim the reward.'

There was a muted exchange with another person in the room as Marcus and Festus crept closer, sticking to the wall as they edged towards the entrance to the triclinium. As they reached the corner Festus held his hand up to stop Marcus, then eased himself forward and peered round before moving back into the shadows of the corridor.

'Three of them,' he said softly. 'Two men and a woman. No one else. We're in luck. When I give the word we move in quickly. We'll deal with the other man and I'll handle Decimus while you take care of the woman. Keep her guarded and keep her quiet.'

'I can handle Decimus.'

'I know you can. But we need him alive.'

Marcus felt a surge of anger. 'I know that.'

'Marcus, hate can turn a person's mind. Make them do something they know they shouldn't. It's better we don't take the risk. Now, draw your sword.'

Marcus swallowed his feelings and eased his blade from his scabbard as Festus readied another arrow. 'Ready?'

Marcus swallowed. 'Ready.'

Festus rose up and stepped into the chamber, Marcus hurrying forward at his side. It was a large space, some fifteen paces across and thirty or so in length, with couches and low tables arranged round a large open space. At the far end three people were seated round a table, on which several silver trays carried the remains of a meal. Their backs were towards Festus and Marcus. Decimus, instantly recognizable from his bald head, sat in the middle. To his left lay Thermon in a plain black tunic. To his right lay a thin woman in a finely embroidered green stola. She had ornately styled dark hair. At first the diners ignored the sound of light footsteps and then Decimus turned to look over his shoulder as he spoke harshly.

'I did not send for . . . What the?'

Thermon looked up and instantly sprang to his feet, lowering into a crouch as he snatched up a knife from the table. Festus stopped, fifteen feet away, took aim and loosed an arrow. The shaft blurred through the air as Thermon leapt to one side. The woman let out a cry of shock as the barbed head gashed his shoulder. He sprang forward as Festus frantically tried to fit another arrow. He had only pulled back the arrow a short way before Thermon crashed into him. Even so the arrow pierced the other man's chest as they tumbled on to the floor.

Marcus glanced at Decimus and saw that he was still too shocked to react and then turned to help his friend. Thermon had his weight on top of Festus, the knife clenched in his fist as he strained to stab it into the bodyguard's throat. Festus had a fist clamped round his opponent's wrist, trying to hold the blade off, but inch by inch it drew closer.

Marcus reached the struggling men in an instant and did not hesitate as he slashed his sword into the back of Thermon's skull. He heard the bone crack and Thermon let out a loud grunt, before Festus thrust him away and rolled to one side. Marcus glanced down and saw that Thermon's eyes were blinking wildly as his jaw shuddered. A dark pool of blood was spilling out across the tiled floor round his head.

'He's done for,' said Festus as he drew his sword. 'Let's deal with Decimus.'

Decimus had already grasped the danger he was in and surged up from his couch as he plucked a knife from the table. Without a moment's hesitation he grabbed the woman who had been lying on the couch next to him and spun her round so that she faced the intruders. Clamping one arm across her chest he brought his knife hand up with the point barely an inch from the woman's slender throat. She let out another quick cry of terror and clenched her eyes shut.

'Come any closer, and I'll kill her!' Decimus snarled. 'I mean it!'

Festus gave a dry laugh. 'We've come for you, Decimus. Nothing's going to stop us.'

'Come for me?' Now it was Decimus who laughed. 'Nonsense. You've come for that boy's mother.'

At his words the woman opened her eyes and Marcus focused his attention fully on her for the first time since they had entered the room. As he recognized her familiar features he felt the strength drain from his limbs and he lowered his sword in shock.

'Mother . . .'

She gasped and made an impulsive gesture to reach out as she tried to step away from Decimus. 'Marcus . . . My Marcus.'

Decimus wrenched her back harshly. 'Stand still, you bitch! Don't you dare move again, if you want to live.'

Her voice trembled as she spoke. 'You told me that he was being held –'

'Shut up!' Decimus shouted in her ear. 'Shut your mouth!'

Festus lowered his sword and held out his other hand. 'Let her go, Decimus. If you want to live. She's the one we've come for. Let her go, and we'll leave.'

'Ha!' he spat. 'You think me a fool? The moment she's out of my hands I'll end up like Thermon down there.'

Marcus glanced aside and saw Thermon's body twitching as he bled out. Then his eyes snapped back to his mother as he spoke in a clear, cold voice. 'Let her go.'

'I don't think so.' Decimus grinned, then drew a deep breath and called out at the top of his voice. 'Guards! Slaves! On me! Help! Help!'

Marcus and Festus looked on helplessly as he raised the alarm. It was Livia who reacted first. Bunching her fist, she drove her elbow back and up into Decimus's face. There was a light crunch as his nose broke and he let out a gasp of pain and surprise, loosening his grip. With her other hand she snatched at his knife hand and wrestled it away from her throat.

Decimus howled in pain and rage. 'You'll pay for that!'

He punched his spare fist into her stomach and Livia folded up with a light groan, still trying to force the knife away, now with both hands.

'Hold him!' Festus shouted, racing forward. Marcus had already sprung towards them and punched the guard of his sword into Decimus's jaw, snapping his head back. He punched again, quickly, and Decimus's eyes rolled in a daze. Festus dropped his sword and clasped the other man's hands, forcing them away from Livia so that she fell to one side. With a powerful blow, Festus sent the moneylender sprawling on to a couch, and the knife clattered to the floor at his feet. Before either Festus or Marcus could act, they heard a shrill scream of savage rage as Livia snatched up the knife and leapt on to Decimus, stabbing at his throat. Blood sprayed into the air as he tried in vain to ward off her assault.

'Please!' he begged. 'No! Please . . .'

'Animal!' she shrieked. 'Vile murderer! Scum! Pig! Die! DIE!'

Marcus looked on aghast, trembling in grief and fear at the

sight of the mother he had sought for two years – the mother who had loved and nurtured him – bringing the blade up high to strike again. The man stopped pleading as his efforts to protect himself became more feeble, and then his hand flopped at his side. Festus reached out and firmly grasped Livia's right wrist, taking the knife from her.

Decimus lay still, silenced, sprawled on the floor in his blood-drenched tunic.

'That's enough,' Festus said gently. 'Enough. He's dead.'

'D-dead?' she mumbled, then lowered her head as her shoulders heaved. Her bloodied fingers opened and the blade dropped on to Decimus's chest. Then she pulled herself off the body and turned towards Marcus. Dark strands of her hair mingled with the red flecks on her face as she cried.

Before Marcus knew what he was doing he had his arms about her and drew her head into his chest, feeling her shudder as she wept and held him tightly. He felt overcome with a seething mixture of emotions – love, relief, grief and tenderness. He recalled the times that she had held him this way when he was younger, to comfort him when he was hurt or afraid, and his heart swelled with devotion to his mother.

'Marcus . . . My boy . . . My child.' Her voice was raw as she gasped the words through her tears.

'We have to go,' Festus interrupted. 'Now. Before anyone comes to see what all the shouting was about. Back the way we came.'

He helped Livia to her feet and Marcus steadied her with his arm as they headed for the corridor. Festus remained by the body. He took one last look at Decimus, then stepped towards the nearest of the stands that carried the oil lamps lighting the room, knocking it to the ground. He did the same to the others as he followed Marcus and his mother. As pools of burning oil spilled out, the flames caught on to the rich fabrics covering the couches, eagerly spreading as the fire took hold of the furniture.

Making their way down the corridor, they saw the slaves emerge from the kitchen, their anxious expressions illuminated by the flames in the room behind the dark outline of the three people heading towards them.

'Fire!' Festus shouted. 'There's a fire! Run!'

The slaves hesitated for an instant before the first turned and ran back into the kitchen. His companions followed, leaving Marcus and the others to reach the kitchen unopposed. They hurried through it, and down the service corridor to the slave quarters. By the time they reached the small courtyard it was filled with slaves looking up at the orange hue in the high windows of the villa's banqueting hall. The crackle of the blaze was clearly audible and the first brilliant tongues of flame pierced the wooden window frames.

Marcus ignored them as he helped his mother out through the gate. Lupus was waiting outside, sword poised until he saw that it was his friends. His relieved expression quickly gave way to anxiety as he looked at Livia.

'Is she all right?'

'I'm fine,' she replied and turned to smile at Marcus. 'Really.'

'No time for this,' Festus interrupted. 'We have to hide these bodies behind the woodpile and escape as fast as we can. Lupus, help me. Marcus, get your mother away from here. Down there, in the trees.' Marcus steered his mother across the grass meadow and the others hurried after him a moment later as the flames began to burst through the roof of the villa, casting long, flickering shadows ahead of the figures fleeing into the night.

22

In the morning there was a clear view from across the valley of the devastation caused by the fire. Smoke still trailed up into the blue sky from the blackened ruins of Decimus's villa. Small groups of curious onlookers were walking up from the town towards the estate. Festus had left the cave at first light to make his way into Tegea to purchase rations and find out what the accepted explanation was about the cause of the fire. If suspicions had been aroused, then they would have to leave Tegea as swiftly as possible.

With Festus gone, Marcus was left to keep watch. Both his mother and Lupus were still asleep in the shadows at the rear of the cave, but the light from the morning sun would soon wake them. Cerberus lay at his side, head resting between his huge paws and his eyes all but closed as his nostrils stirred with each easy breath. As Marcus looked round at his mother, curled up in a ball with her back to him, he felt confused.

He had lived for this moment ever since the time they were parted when she had begged him to make his escape alone. He had dreamt about rescuing her and eagerly anticipated the release of all the love and longing that he had been forced to bottle up inside. Behind it all had been the desire to return his life to the way things were before. He had always considered that to be his aim, without ever really questioning if it was likely to happen.

Now that he and his mother were free again, the future suddenly seemed uncertain. Not only was a return to the farm fraught with difficulties, but he had changed. He had grown up during the last two years and was now more a man than a boy. And he knew that his mother had changed too. Although Marcus was overjoyed to be reunited with her, his emotions were confused. After all, she had butchered a man in front of him. And there had been the shock of finding her dining alongside the man Marcus knew as a bitter enemy. Back in Athens, Decimus had taunted him with the image of his mother in chains and starving. That was a lie, Marcus realized, told to make his misery as acute as possible. He cursed the moneylender under his breath before his thoughts returned to the previous night.

After their escape from the villa she had clutched him tightly as she sobbed. Then, as Festus urged her to put aside her feelings and escape, she had become silent and withdrawn. They had sat in silence, side by side, with their backs to the rock as they watched the flames devouring the villa. The lurid red of the fire bathed the surrounding landscape and the roar of the flames carried clearly in the still night air. Eventually, as the fire began to die down they had both fallen asleep, curled up next to one another as they had done sometimes when he was a small boy.

Turning back to resume his watch over the approaches to the cave, Marcus wondered how Festus was getting on. They would need food for the road now that the bodyguard was keen to put some distance between them and Tegea, without attracting any attention along the way. He hoped the fire would be regarded as a tragic accident for Decimus and Thermon. With luck their bodies, and those of the guards they had disposed of, would have burned sufficiently to conceal the wounds, and in the shock of the blaze no one would recall the small band of fugitives fleeing into the darkness.

'A sestertius for your thoughts.'

Marcus turned sharply to see that his mother had stirred and was sitting up watching him. She smiled uncertainly and stood up, then trod lightly across the floor of the cave in order not to wake Lupus, and sat down beside Marcus.

'My poor Marcus.' She put her arm round him and drew him towards her. 'My poor boy. I had always hoped that one day I might escape from Decimus and try to find you.' She smiled uncertainly at him. 'But it was you who found me. No longer the child I knew. You've become a young man . . . You remind me of your father.' Tears glistened in her eyes and she quickly kissed his forehead. They sat in silence for a moment and Marcus felt her stifling a sob. There was so much he wanted to tell her, so much he wanted to ask, but he did not know where to begin. She sensed his uneasiness and drew back a little to look at him. 'What are you thinking?'

Marcus sighed heavily. 'I'm not sure. The only thing that I lived for over the last two years was to find you. I had to save you. I thought you were being held in chains and worked to death. I wasn't prepared to see you in that room. At his table, eating at his side . . .'

His mother was silent for a moment. 'Does it matter? We are free, that's what counts. What do you think has been keeping me alive while we have been apart, Marcus? I lived for the same thing. I did what I had to do in order to survive, and, so I thought, to keep you safe from harm.'

He looked at her. 'What do you mean?'

She frowned briefly and her bottom lip trembled before she swallowed and continued. 'Decimus told me that his men had recaptured you after we were separated. He said that you were taken to his house in Athens to serve as a slave there. As long as I did what he asked, you would be safe from harm.'

Marcus fought to control a new wave of hatred for Decimus. The man had deserved to die. Even now that he was dead, the suffering he had inflicted on them continued, with an agonizing new twist. He had lied to them both, using his lies to force his mother to do his bidding.

'I'm glad that it was you who killed him,' he said harshly. 'You deserved vengeance more than me.'

She looked at him in surprise. 'No. I don't think so. Decimus stole your childhood. Nothing can make up for that. And now I see that you are no longer my young son.' She examined his features in detail for the first time by the light of day. 'You have grown. You look strong and there is a hard glint to your eyes. You have changed,' she concluded sadly and shook her head as if reluctant to accept her judgement. 'Changed . . . You will never be the same Marcus I knew, the one I had frozen in time during every moment of the last two years.'

Marcus felt tears fill his eyes and took her hand and squeezed it. 'I am your son, Mother. I always will be. I owe my very life to you and swear by all that is sacred that I will protect you. We will never be separated again. Not now.'

Marcus's mother smiled. 'We must try not to let the past ruin what we have. We must do what all free people do, and live in hope. We are free and our fate is our own to decide again. Hold on to that, my dear Marcus. Hold on to that and move on. Don't let the shadow of Decimus linger over us.'

'I'll try. But it won't be easy.'

'It never is, living with the past,' she said with feeling. 'I know, believe me. It was the same when I lived with your father . . .' She glanced at him quickly before she continued. 'Titus.'

Marcus felt a nervous tremor ripple down his spine. He knew that the time had come to let his mother know that he had learned the truth about the identity of his real father. He shifted so that he could face her. 'Mother,' he said, 'I know about Spartacus.'

He reached a hand up and patted the material of his tunic over the brand on his shoulder. 'I know about this, and what it means.'

Marcus's mother had paled. Her expression filled with fear.

'You know?' she repeated. 'By the Gods, Marcus, how did you ever find out? Who told you?'

'After we were separated I was taken to a gladiator school in Capua for training. There was a man there who saw the brand and recognized it. He told me.'

She closed her eyes and spoke softly. 'They made you into a gladiator . . . The Gods could not be more cruel. Your father suffered the same fate. He swore he would dedicate his life to making sure no other man ever had to suffer that. And now his son, his only son, has had to endure the very thing that tormented his soul every day that he led the fight against Rome.' She breathed in deeply. 'Is there no end to it? No end to our suffering?'

She looked at him again. 'What was the name of the man who told you about Spartacus?'

Marcus heard the pain in her voice as she spoke the name. He swallowed before he replied. 'Brixus.'

She looked blank for a moment and then smiled warmly. 'Brixus. He survived then. That's good. He was one of the best. He would have died at the side of Spartacus if he had been fit enough to fight in that last, terrible battle where it all ended. I'm glad he is still alive. So few of us were spared when they rounded up the prisoners.' Her eyes suddenly glinted. 'And yet they failed to extinguish the blaze that Spartacus started. There is still a spark of hope that will one day light the beacon and signal to every slave that the rebellion lives on. You are that beacon, Marcus.'

Marcus had come to know that slavery was a crushing burden and those who lived under it endured a constant black despair like a dark, bottomless pit. It filled him with a sense of unspeakable horror. With a flash of insight, Marcus grasped the powerful force that had driven Spartacus to revolt against slavery, despite the terrible risks and great odds that faced him. *What depths of courage he must have possessed*, Marcus thought. To not only take on Rome, but to confront the meaning of slavery every day. To carry in his heart a full awareness of the horror that slavery entailed. It was that knowledge that had driven Spartacus to fight Rome, right up until he drew his last breath. Marcus felt a sense of awe for the man who had fathered him and began to understand the depth of devotion from his followers – men like Brixus and Mandracus who had kept the flame of rebellion burning and fed the hope that all slaves silently guarded like a treasure.

Marcus began to see a new future now that he was reunited with his mother. He could not return to the life he had lost. That path was closed to him now. He had grown beyond that and there was a burden he must shoulder, like his father before him. There was a struggle against a monstrous injustice in which he must take part. And there was no alternative to that struggle other than the shame of bowing down before the greatest evil known to humanity. At last he understood his father's heart and for the first time saw the dim features of the face of his father in his mind's eye. The careworn strain in his expression, the determination in his steely eyes and the faint smile of approval as he knew that he had not died in vain. That the great cause, for which he had given his life, lived on in his only son.

He looked up and met his mother's intense gaze steadily. 'That day may come, Mother. But only when the moment is right. And only if I choose to continue my father's fight. You said we should not let the past rule us. Well, I believe that. I am free. I am not the slave of any other man, and I am not the slave of any other man's dream.'

Marcus's mother opened her mouth as if to protest, but no words came. At length she shook her head and looked down. 'You are right. Your father would be proud of you, as I am proud of you.'

Marcus embraced the words, warmth spreading through his heart.

'Do your friends know?'

'Lupus does. He learned the truth from Brixus later on.'

'And the man, Festus?'

Marcus shook his head. 'I dare not tell him.'

'Why not?'

'I met Festus after I was bought from the owner of the gladiator school. At the time Festus was serving as the leader of Julius Caesar's bodyguards.'

Her eyes opened wide, staring. 'Caesar? Then . . . then we're in terrible danger. We have to get out of here, Marcus. Before he returns from the town.'

'No. Festus is my friend. I don't think we have anything to fear from him.'

Cerberus suddenly stirred and his ears perked up as a low growl rumbled in his throat. A twig cracked on the path leading up past the cave and Marcus quietly drew his sword, indicating to his mother to get to the back of the cave, taking the dog with her. She slipped her hand into Cerberus's collar and crept back towards the still slumbering Lupus. Marcus moved to a rock at the side of the cave mouth and crouched down out of sight. His ears strained to pick up any more sounds and a moment later he heard the crunch of boots drawing closer. They grew louder in volume then stopped for a beat.

'Marcus?'

He felt a surge of relief as he recognized Festus's voice and stood up, sheathing his sword before he stepped out on to the path. Caesar's bodyguard stood staring at him with an intense expression. He carried a net bag over his shoulder and swung it carefully to the ground, revealing the contents: bread, cheese and fruit. His hand released the end of the bag and Festus rested it on the handle of his dagger. In his other hand he held a thin wooden board on which a notice had been painted.

'I think you should see this, Marcus.'

He held it up for him to read.

Wanted for the MURDER of Procrustes, a citizen of Leuctra. Authorities are looking for MARCUS, a boy of approximately 13 years, travelling with TWO accomplices, a boy answering to the name of LUPUS and a man named FESTUS. Marcus has brown hair, brown eyes, of average height for his age, but better built. He has a distinguishing scar on his shoulder. A brand, in the shape of a sword piercing the head of a wolf. A reward of 10,000 denarii is offered by Governor Servillus for their capture.

Marcus looked up and saw the cold expression in the man's face as he spoke. 'I found this in the market square. There are more like it in every public space in Tegea. Would you care to tell me why you think Governor Servillus is prepared to offer such a huge fortune to get his hands on you?'

'I-I have no idea.'

'Don't lie to me, Marcus. You'd better tell me what is going on. You'd better tell me what that mark on your shoulder means. I saw that look on the official's face back in the arena. He recognized the mark. He knew it meant something important. So you'd better tell me about it. Right now. I want to hear the truth, all of it, from your own lips, Marcus.'

He took a step towards Marcus as he tightened his grip on the handle of his dagger.

23

'It is the mark of Spartacus,' Livia said as she emerged from the rear of the cave. 'It is the mark that was placed on his son many years ago.'

She stepped forward, between Festus and Marcus, and he saw that she also carried a sword, taken from the packs at the rear of the cave. She raised it and pointed it at Festus. 'Marcus is also my son. He is all I have in the world. I have lost the man I loved, and the man I came close to loving. I have lost my home, my dignity and almost every shred of the will to go on. I will die before I let you harm Marcus.'

As she spoke, Cerberus padded out of the cave and stood by Marcus's side. Sensing the tension between the humans, he lowered his head and let out a low growl as the hairs on the back of his neck rose.

Festus stood still, his expression unreadable as he stared at Livia and then Marcus. 'The son of Spartacus. The greatest threat that Rome has ever faced on our own soil. A bitter enemy of my master, Julius Caesar, and all Romans . . . including me.'

Marcus did not like the flat tone of his voice. He knew well enough how swiftly the bodyguard could spring into action and how lethal he could be with a weapon in his hand. So he drew his sword again and braced his muscles to react the instant Festus made a hostile move. But the man did not move as he pursed his lips and his brow creased into a puzzled frown.

'By rights I should strike you down here and now. While you live there are bound to be fools who will take up arms against their masters the moment they hear that the standard of Spartacus has been raised once again.'

Livia raised the sword. 'If you even think about it, I will cut you down.'

Festus glanced at her and cocked an eyebrow. 'Really? Do you think I could not kill you before you laid a scratch on me? Lower the sword and back away. I won't warn you again.'

Marcus kept his eyes fixed on Festus as he spoke quietly and urgently. 'Mother, do as he says. Please.'

She hesitated, the point of the sword wavering in the air

between herself and Festus. Then she shook her head. 'I won't let him harm you, Marcus. I'd die before that happens.'

Festus smiled coldly. 'You will certainly die before that happens, unless you back off.'

Marcus reached out with his left hand to take her sword arm and eased it away from the bodyguard. Then he placed himself in front of her, directly opposite Festus, no more than two sword lengths away.

'Festus, there will be no new slave revolt. I will not raise my father's standard. There would be no point in doing it when there is no hope of success. Brixus wanted to use me to provoke a new rebellion when I was held in his camp last winter, but I refused. You have nothing to fear from me, Festus. All I want is to live out my life in freedom, and take care of my mother. Would you really stand in the way of such a simple desire? Do you really want to hand me over to the most powerful men in Rome so that they can parade me and my mother through the streets in chains before executing us in front of a howling mob? Festus, I have fought at your side. We have faced great dangers together in the last few months. Just a few hours ago you risked your life to save my mother. Does none of that mean anything to you?'

'That was all before I discovered who you really are,' Festus growled. 'You have betrayed me, Marcus. After everything that we have been through. I risked my life for you, and, as you say, we have fought side by side. I thought of you as a friend. More than a friend. And now it seems I have never really known you at all.' Festus took a step towards Marcus. 'So great a secret.' He shook his head. 'So great the possible consequences for Rome . . . And for me.'

'Festus —' Marcus began.

'No!' Festus spat. 'I will not listen. I am Caesar's man . . . If I let you go then I betray my master and turn my back on all the years that I have protected him and his interests. In the end I turn my back on Rome.'

But as Marcus watched his friend, his body seemed to sag, and he sighed wearily. 'And yet . . . A bond has been forged between us, Marcus. When you arrived at Caesar's house in Rome, I thought you no more than a typical young gladiator, a violent, thoughtless thug, and I admit I resented having you placed in my charge, no matter that Caesar said you had potential. But you proved me wrong. I came to see that you have courage, quick wits and a good heart. In time I regarded you as a comrade, a friend, and in the last few months as a son. A son any man would be proud to call his own.' He looked earnestly at Marcus and the boy felt burdened with guilt.

'Festus, I'm sorry – I would have told you, if I could. But don't you understand? I knew it would be putting you in a terrible position, and I was worried for my life.'

'You could have told me before I found out for myself.'

'Would that have made any difference?' Marcus asked.

Festus paused and shrugged lightly. 'I don't know. It might . . . Does Lupus know?'

'He does,' Marcus admitted. 'He discovered the truth from Brixus and I swore him to secrecy.'

Marcus saw a flicker of pain cross the bodyguard's face. Marcus swallowed nervously. 'It wasn't my choice to tell him, Festus. But I must know – what do you intend to do, since you know the truth?'

Festus shook his head, and sighed.

'I too swore an oath, Marcus. To serve Caesar and obey his orders. And he ordered me to accompany and protect you, and do all that I could to help you find and rescue your mother, then escort you both to safety.'

He gestured towards the board carrying the offer of a reward for Marcus. 'Now it seems that my job is not complete. You are in danger, and I will not have carried out Caesar's orders until I am certain that both you and your mother are out of danger.'

It was all Marcus could do not to collapse with gratitude and relief. He realized he had been holding his breath, his whole body rigid with tension. He had feared that he would have to fight for his life against the man who had trained him. A fight he would almost certainly have lost. Now, that peril seemed to have passed.

He felt a spark of hope as he cleared his throat. 'So?'

'So we must get away from here, as soon as possible.'

'I know. I wanted to return to my home.'

'No, Marcus. You cannot return there. You cannot return to that life. It is closed to you, and has been from the moment you were torn from it.'

'Then where shall we go?' Livia asked helplessly.

'As far from here as possible. Far from Greece and far from Rome. Somewhere no one will know you and you can both be safe. Only then will my orders be satisfied and I will have been true to my honour.'

Marcus glanced at his mother and they shared a look of relief before he turned back to the bodyguard, sheathed his sword and extended his hand. 'Thank you.'

Festus sighed and stepped forward to grasp Marcus's hand. 'You are making me pay a heavy price, Marcus. Forcing me to choose between Caesar and you. Before we met I'd never have questioned the bond between a master and his servant. Now?

288

Now I have learned that the bond between comrades is stronger. Caesar will never forgive me when he discovers the truth.'

Marcus detected the sadness in the man's tone and felt a stab of guilt that he was placing someone he respected and regarded with affection in danger.

Festus stared at Marcus. 'One thing. Never hide the truth from me again, Marcus. I have earned that right.'

'Very well.'

They stood quietly, each staring at the other, almost as if they had only just met and were sizing each other up for the first time.

'What's going on then?' a voice interrupted, and Lupus walked stiffly out of the cave, scratching his head. He saw the bag of bread and cheese on the ground and his face lit up. 'Oh, good! I'm starving. Well, what are we waiting for? Let's tuck in!'

Festus decided that they must leave the cave as soon as they had finished eating. There had been little said and Lupus glanced curiously at his companions as they ate, clearly confused by what had happened while he was asleep. Then he caught sight of the placard resting against the side of the cave and he sat, a chunk of bread halfway to his mouth as his jaw sagged open. He glanced at Festus, the blood draining from his face. The effect was so comical that Marcus could not help laughing. He choked on the mouthful that he had been eating and Festus slapped him hard on the back to help clear his throat. Cerberus growled at the bodyguard before anxiously nuzzling his master's face. The tension disappeared as Festus and Lupus chuckled at Marcus and his dog, while Livia looked on with a smile.

'It's all right,' Marcus gasped, eyes watering. 'Festus knows the truth.'

'What? How?'

'He guessed some of it, and I told him the rest. No more secrets now.'

Festus nodded. 'And that's the way it will stay. If you and I are to get Marcus and his mother to safety, then we must look out for each other. All of us. I won't lie to any of you. The gravest dangers still lie ahead of us. Now the Roman authorities have discovered that Spartacus had a son, they will not rest until Marcus is captured or killed. The only advantage we have is that they can't afford to release the information.'

'Why not?' asked Lupus.

Marcus intervened. 'Because if word of it got out, they would fear that every slave in the empire was waiting for the chance to rise against their masters.'

'Precisely,' said Festus. 'Better to deal with the problem

quietly. That means they will have to be careful as they hunt for you. It'll be a game of cat and mouse.'

Marcus nodded grimly.

His mother sighed. 'Then it's going to be a long journey. Wherever it takes us.' She looked down at the ground between her sandals. 'Our troubles are far from over.'

Marcus gently took her hand and gave it a comforting squeeze. 'The worst is behind us, Mother. And whatever dangers we may have to face in the days to come, at least we shall face them together. I'll be there to protect you.'

She looked up with a sad expression. 'That's what I always wanted to do for you. And I have been tormented by the thought that when you most needed protecting I was helpless to do anything.'

'It wasn't your fault. It was Decimus. And now he's paid the price.'

'Yes . . . Yes, at least that's true.'

Festus brushed the crumbs from his tunic and stood up. 'Time we were moving. I want to be as far from Tegea as possible before the end of the day.'

'Where will we go?' Marcus asked.

'West, to the coast. And then we take a ship far from Greece and Italy.'

The others stood up and Cerberus wagged his tail, looking at each of them in turn. Once their packs were fastened and slung from their shoulders Festus gestured towards the path and set off. Lupus followed him, and then Marcus and his mother, with the dog trotting at their heels. Away to their left the smoke still trailed up into the sky above the estate of Decimus. It was like the smoke from an offering to the Gods, Marcus reflected. The kind of offering that sailors and other travellers made before a long journey to keep them safe and ensure that they reached their destination safely.

He smiled at the thought, and glanced at his mother.

His heart filled with a warmth he had not known for years.

It all started with a Scarecrow.

Puffin is seventy years old.
Sounds ancient, doesn't it? But Puffin has never been
so lively. We're always on the lookout for the next big
idea, which is how it began all those years ago.

Penguin Books was a big idea from the mind of
a man called Allen Lane, who in 1935 invented
the quality paperback and changed the world.
**And from great Penguins, great Puffins grew,
changing the face of children's books forever.**

The first four Puffin Picture Books were hatched in 1940 and the
first Puffin story book featured a man with broomstick arms called
Worzel Gummidge. In 1967 Kaye Webb, Puffin Editor, started the
Puffin Club, promising to **'make children into readers'**.
She kept that promise and over 200,000 children became
devoted Puffineers through their quarterly instalments of
Puffin Post, which is now back for a new generation.

Many years from now, we hope you'll look back and
remember Puffin with a smile. **No matter what your age
or what you're into, there's a Puffin for everyone.**
The possibilities are endless, but one thing is for sure:
whether it's a picture book or a paperback, a sticker book
or a hardback, **if it's got that little Puffin
on it – it's bound to be good.**